I0651744

John Campbell

Narrative by Major-General John Campbell

John Campbell

Narrative by Major-General John Campbell

ISBN/EAN: 9783337367077

Printed in Europe, USA, Canada, Australia, Japan

Cover: Foto ©Andreas Hilbeck / pixelio.de

More available books at **www.hansebooks.com**

NARRATIVE

BY

MAJOR-GENERAL JOHN CAMPBELL,

C.B.

OF HIS OPERATIONS

IN

THE HILL TRACTS OF ORISSA

FOR

THE SUPPRESSION OF HUMAN SACRIFICES AND FEMALE INFANTICIDE.

Printed for Private Circulation.

LONDON:

HURST AND BLACKETT,

13, GREAT MARLBOROUGH STREET.

1861.

PREFACE.

In presenting the following imperfect
sketch of my humble labours in the Khond
country, for the perusal of my friends, I
disclaim all pretension of doing anything
more than offering a plain, unvarnished
statement of what I saw and did. I have
only in my possession fragments of official
Reports, and some private memoranda, to
guide me—but I can safely assert, that the
information, so far as it goes, may be fully
relied on.

I look back with unfeigned gratification
and thankfulness at having been the in-
strument used to accomplish a great and

good work, and I owe much to that illustrious statesman, the late Marquis of Dalhousie, Governor-General of India, who took the liveliest interest in this enterprise of civilization and humanity, and gave it, on every occasion, his powerful and generous support.

By the most Noble the Marquis of Tweedale, when Governor and Commander-in-Chief of Madras, the most cordial sympathy was manifested, and from this distinguished nobleman I never failed to receive the most convincing proofs of the deep interest he felt in all our operations for the Suppression of Human Sacrifices, and Female Infanticide in the Hill Tracts of Orissa.

CONTENTS.

———

CHAPTER I.

CHAPTER II.

CHAPTER III.

CHAPTER IV.

CHAPTER V.

CHAPTER VI.

CHAPTER VII.

CHAPTER VIII.

CHAPTER IX.

CHAPTER X.

NARRATIVE.

CHAPTER I.

INTRODUCTION—SOME ACCOUNT OF THE DISTRICT, OR ZE-
MINDARY OF GOOMSUR—THE VICISSITUDES OF THE
RAJAH.

So little is known in England of the
wild mountain tribes inhabiting the Hill
tracts of the ancient kingdom of Orissa,
and still less of the barbarous practices
which prevailed amongst them, that I have
ventured, at the special request of several
esteemed friends, to compile a brief narra·
tive of the efforts which have been made to

suppress the cruel rite of human sacrifice, which annually doomed to a frightful and bloody death hundreds of victims, as also to check the revolting practice of female infanticide, which deprived of life, almost in the very hour of their birth, between seven and eight hundred female children.

Between the Mahanuddy river, which empties itself into the Bay of Bengal, near to Cuttack, and the river Godavery to the south, the country is divided into some forty or fifty petty principalities, ruled over by chiefs of "Ooryah" caste. These chieftains of Orissa are undoubtedly of very ancient origin. They claim for themselves a fabulous descent, each great family bearing as his coat-of-arms the animal or object from which his ancestors sprung. Thus, for example, the rajah, or prince and ruler

of Goomsur had a peacock; another prince
had a snake; another a bamboo tree, and
such armorial bearings are no small source
of vanity and pride.

These various petty rulers are generally
uneducated and devoid of all mental cul-
ture. Many, from early debauchery and
unbridled indulgence of their passions, become completely imbecile. Indeed, amongst
this class of men, imbecility and feebleness
of character is the general rule. The state
exacts from each of these rulers an annual
tribute, varying from one to eight thousand
pounds. It usually happens that this tribute money is in arrears. The state presses
for payment, and if the rajah cannot raise
the amount, his estate is frequently administered for him by the revenue officers
of government, until the debt due is cleared
off: but if the arrears be very heavy, then

it is sold to liquidate the amount due. The government is most generally the purchaser.

I will, in as few words as possible, sketch the history of one of these little palatinates, and I select that of " Goomsur," because it was owing to the deposition of the reigning prince, and the annexation of his country to the British dominions, that we first became acquainted with the fact of human victims being sacrificed on the altar of a bloody superstition.

The little principality of " Goomsur" reckons about four hundred square miles, one half of which is primeval forest, the other cleared and well cultivated. In 1783, its ruler was named Rajah Vikramah Bunge, and the yearly tribute demanded from him was five thousand pounds. He failed to fulfil his engagements, and consequently

was deprived of his estate, and his brother
Lutshmunnah Bunge substituted.   He
agreed to pay double the amount required
from his brother, and placed himself and
kingdom entirely under the control of
native bankers and money dealers, who became his security for the due payment of
the tribute.   This man died, leaving his
son, Streckarah Bunge, to reign in his stead.
Very chequered was the existence of this
native prince.   Disgusted at first with the
state of affairs, and slightly fanatical, he
abdicated in favour of his son, Dhunagi
Bunge, and made a pilgrimage to some
holy shrine: but after a few years' absence,
he returned, expelled his son, resumed the
reins of government, and boldly bid defiance to the paramount power by refusing
to pay any tribute at all.

Necessarily this challenge was not long

unanswered, and the government troops soon gave a good account of this unruly rajah, who once more became a private gentleman—the supreme government having determined to replace his son Dhunagi Bunge at the head of affairs. In fact, this harassed district was in a constant state of oscillation between father and son, who alternately reigned and were disposed. Thus Dhunagi Bunge 'had not long been reinstated, when, in consequence of the commission of atrocious crimes, it was found absolutely necessary again to depose, and further to incarcerate him. Then came the father's turn again, but like other illustrious princes, he had in exile neither learnt nor forgotten anything; and after a very short possession of power, he failed to pay the stipulated tribute, and expiated his offences in exile in a distant country. Once more the government gave the son Dhunagi Bunge a chance of retrieving his past errors, he was brought back from confinement and re-installed as ruler of Goomsur. With common prudence he might have been ruler to this hour, but he boldly hoisted the standard of rebellion, paid no tribute, and betook himself and his establishment to those mountain fastnesses where dwell the various tribes of Khonds, who owe and yield a certain ill-defined allegiance to the lowland ruler, of which I will speak again hereafter.

Then ended the eventful career of this man and his family. The government of India determined on the complete subjugation of the country. A large force under General Taylor was employed for that purpose, and the Hon. Mr. Russell was named as the political agent, with very extensive

powers. I was appointed an assistant and
also secretary to Mr. Russell, and took an
active part during the whole campaign
which extended over two years. The unhappy rajah was hunted from place to
place, and finally died at a little mountain fortress. The whole country became part of the British territory, whatever
members of the Bunge family remained
were made state prisoners, and a campaign
of almost unexampled severity terminated
in the accomplishment of all the objects of
the government.

CHAPTER II.

THE harassing operations to which I have referred in the preceding chapter, first brought us into contact with the wild and warlike races of Khond tribes, who dwell on the table land of the great chain of mountain ranges which extend nearly north and south from the Mahanuddy to the Godavery.

These mountains are about one hundred and fifty to two hundred miles distant from the sea, and from two to three thousand feet above it. Their steep and rugged sides are densely covered with the bamboo, damur, and other common Indian trees. Game of all kinds abound, and the larger description of animals, tigers, panthers, bears, wild buffaloes, &c., are numerous.

The means of access to these highland regions are most difficult. Steep narrow winding paths through the ravines conduct to the mountain table-land, and the ascent is equally wearisome and troublesome. When at last the summit is reached, the eye beholds a well-watered, open country, producing abundantly rice, oil seeds, turmeric, and sometimes large crops of dhall, (a kind of pea) and millet. The Khonds know nothing of the science of agriculture; they exhaust the soil with crops without intermission, then abandon their fields to become again a forest, and clear fresh jungle land for future crops.

These Hill tribes in no one way resemble the inhabitants of the plains, whence, I should judge, they had been driven by the successive conquering races whose descendants now occupy them. Hence we find in their language, though a dialect entirely of itself, words evidently having both a Telingah, Canarese, and Ooryah origin.

The inhabitants of the Orissa range of hills are chiefly called "Khonds," "Gonds," and "Sowrahs;" the two latter races are not addicted to the practice of human sacrifice. The language of the Sowrahs is distinct from that of the Khond tribes. This narrative has almost exclusive reference to the Khonds.

Khond communities are divided into districts and villages. A community is formed

of a union of villages, called a "Mootah,"
and these again united, form a district.
Each village has its own chief or "Mulleko,"
and also an officer called "Digaloo" or in-
terpreter, of the "Panoo" caste, a race
very useful to the Khond tribes, who regard
them as in every way their inferior. The
"Panoo" is the man of business of the
Khond, who holds it beneath his dignity to
barter or to traffic, and regards as plebeians
all who are not warriors or tillers of the
soil.

Districts again are governed by a chief of
Ooryah extraction, called "Bissoi," the
descendant usually of some daring adven-
turer, whose fallen fortunes drove him to
the hills, where, with his band of followers,
he received a cordial welcome from the
mountain tribes. The Khonds regarded
such a warrior more capable to rule over

them, and more fit to lead them on in battle, than one of their own tribe.

Their villages vary in size from twenty to eighty houses, well and substantially built of planks split from the damur tree, and rudely fashioned into shape with an axe. The roof is of bamboo, thatched over with grass. One long street usually forms the village, which has at either end a rough palisade. Clusters of villages are always built together both for defence and cultivation.

Rice is the great staple of cultivation, and great pains are bestowed thereon. The fields are formed in a succession of terraces to which water, when available, is conducted with no mean skill. Near the villages tobacco is invariably grown, a rough, coarse, strong leaf, indispensable however to gratify the Khond appetite. Their implements of husbandry are most primitive. Their wooden plough, drawn by buffaloes, or else small oxen, merely scratches the ground.

Their breed of cattle is very inferior. In their mountains goats abound, but few sheep. The Khonds do not use milk, but can assign no reason for their abstinence.

They have a passion for the chase. Their hunting season opens in the hot months, about April, which is the period when they burn the underwood and rank grass of the jungles, and this operation drives the wild animals from their lairs to seek a refuge in the unburnt forest. They are then pursued by the Khonds, who are exceedingly expert at tracking game. If in hunting, an elk, or other large game is wounded, the measure of his "gottira" or slot is taken, and they have an admitted right to pursue him to any distance, even beyond their own boundaries, until it is killed or captured. A division of the quarry is then made in accordance with well established usage, so much to the hunters, so much to the villagers on whose land it has been killed, and on some occasions the rajah, or low-country chief receives a portion.

In the event of any dispute regarding the identity of the pursued animal, the measure of the first slot is produced and received as conclusive.

The hunting season is one of universal revelry and drunkenness. Marriages are usually celebrated at this time, and throughout every district is heard the sound of their rude shrill musical instruments. I should have mentioned that the bow and

arrow and battle-axe are the hunting weapons employed.

It is somewhat singular that the Khond
tribes have never adopted the matchlock,
sword, or shield, which are always carried
by their Ooryah chief, or " Bissoi," and his
followers, and are so superior to the Khond
weapons.

The Khonds generally are an active race,
wiry and lithesome in make, and but im-
perfectly acquainted with the value of
cleanliness. They drink deeply, and obtain
a very intoxicating liquid from the fer-
mented juice of the feathery palm, and also
from the " mowah" tree. They largely
out-number all other classes, and are the
acknowledged lords of the soil. Next in
importance is the Panoo caste, and then the
Ooryah followers of the district chief.

Their clothing consists merely of a few

yards of coarse cotton cloth bound round
the loins, ornamented with a separate piece
striped with red, and dangling down be-
hind like a tail. Their thick black hair
wound round and round their heads is fastened in front by a knot, over which is tied
a strip of red or other cloth. In their
hair they invariably stick three or four
cigars, very simply formed by rolling a
green leaf into a conical shape, and fill-
ing it with their coarse chopped tobacco
leaf.

It is only, however, when they go out
to battle, and tribe meets tribe in hostile
array, that they adorn themselves with all
their finery. Then they swathe their heads
in thick folds of cotton cloth, with pea-
cocks' feathers waving in defiance, cover
their bodies with pieces of skins of bears or
elks; and proud indeed is the warrior who

c

can sport over all a couple of yards of red cloth.

I once witnessed two tribes, each numbering about three hundred men, drawn up in battle array. On this occasion, I prevented any serious results. They had already been three days engaged in the preliminaries of the fight, for many ceremonies are gone through ere comes the tug of war.

Champions from either side perform war dances between the hostile armies; these dances are accompanied by offensive and insulting epithets, and each side challenges and abuses the other. At last they are sufficiently excited, and from words the dancers come to blows; then a general *mêlée* ensues, which is rarely attended with great loss of life, and at night the opposing parties draw off to their respective quarters, only to recommence the following day.

The Khond women are as scantily clad as the men. They partake of the prevailing weakness of their sex in their intense love of ornaments and finery. Coloured beads are highly prized and generally used, with a rude and heavy description of brass bracelet worn on their arms and ankles. As a class, they are not good looking, and their standard of morality is not, I regret to say, very elevated ; hence endless quarrels amongst the tribes, who regard the abduction of a woman by a man of another tribe as a common insult to them all, and unless reparation be made to the injured husband, war is declared against the tribe of the abducting party, and all who are more or less distantly connected with the disputants are drawn into the quarrel.

c 2

Many of their marriage customs are peculiar. On one occasion whilst taking an evening ride, I heard loud cries proceeding from a village close at hand. Fearing some serious quarrel, I rode to the spot, and there I saw a man bearing away upon his back something enveloped in an ample covering of scarlet cloth; he was surrounded by twenty or thirty young fellows, and by them protected from the desperate attacks made on him by a party of young women. On seeking an explanation of this novel scene, I was told that the man had just been married, and his precious burthen was his blooming bride, whom he was now conveying to his own village. Her youthful friends, as it appears is the custom, were seeking to regain possession of her, and hurled stones and bamboos at the devoted bridegroom's head, until he reached the confines of his own village. Then the tables were turned, the bride was fairly won, and off her young friends scampered, screaming and laughing, but not relaxing their speed until they reached their own village.

The Khonds are firm believers in magic, and frequently attribute death or misfortunes of any kind to enchantment. They believe that witches have the faculty of transforming themselves into tigers, and are then called "Pulta Bag." This belief is very similar to the superstition of the peasants of Normandy or Brittany, who thought that certain people had power to change themselves into wolves, and very often did so change themselves for the purpose of frightening others and doing mischief. I had heard often of these "Pulta Bags," and one example came under my own observation.

Whilst examining some magisterial cases, I observed a crowd approaching with two women in front, guarded by three or four armed men. In due time they were brought before me, and charged by a Beniah Khond, (one of a tribe of Khonds inhabiting the slopes of the mountains,) with having transformed themselves into tigers killing and carrying off his son. His story was :—" I went in the evening to the jungle near my village accompanied by my son, to gather fire-wood. We were engaged in doing so when a tiger sprung upon my son and carried him off. I pursued, shouting and making as much noise as I could, when suddenly on turning the shoulder of a rock I saw there two women standing on the top of it. The thing was now clear, the " Pulta Bag," alarmed at my shouts and close pursuit, concealed the body of my son and resumed their original shape. I took them prisoners to my village, where they confessed to what I now charge them with, here they are, ask them." I did ask them, and to my surprise both women acknowledged that the Beniah Khond's story was true, they had killed his son, and had power to transform themselves into tigers. Determined to undeceive the people as to this extraordinary belief, I told the women that I would release them on condition of their transforming themselves into tigers in my presence, which, to the horror of my people, they agreed to do if taken to a neighbouring jungle. This I ordered to be done; when seeing no mode of escape, they threw themselves on the ground, imploring mercy and pardon, and confessing the imposture. They stated that they were poor, and lived by imposing on the credulity of the villagers, who supplied them with food and clothing whenever they chose to ask for it, to secure themselves and cattle from their depredations in the form of a "Pulta Bag." Some were convinced of the imposture, but the majority were disappointed that the supposed witches were not burned or drowned.

Of the religion of a people such as the Khonds, who have no written language, it is not easy to speak with precision. I made many efforts to acquire correct information on this point, but I met with so many contradictions and such vagueness and variety of opinion that I abandoned the attempt, satisfied that their so called religion was probably a corruption and admixture of Buddism and Hindooism, or other ancient systems brought from the plains, from whence, as I have already said, the Khonds originally came. Nevertheless, I am aware that a complete system of Mythology has been devised for them, but much has been introduced of which the Khonds know nothing. One thing however is certain, that, saving a very few tribes, they all propitiate their deity, always a malevolent being, with human sacrifices. In the Hill countries of Goomsur and Boad, the human blood is offered to the Earth Goddess, under the effigy of a bird, to obtain abundant crops, to avert calamity, and to insure prosperity in every way.

In Chinna Kimedy hills this deity is represented by an elephant, but the general purposes of the sacrifice are the same.

In the district of Jeypore, the being to be propitiated by human victims is the "blood-red god of battle Manicksoroo." Thus sacrifices are offered on the eve of a battle,

or when a new fort or an important village
is to be built, or when any danger is im-
minent, and, in short, for general bene-
fits.

Independant of the general sacrifices
offered by the community, it is not an
uncommon thing for private individuals to
make special offerings of human beings in
order to secure the attainment of any particular object.

The religion of the Khonds varies in
different parts of the country. There are
tribes, not numerous, who never sacrifice,
and others who destroy their female off-
spring, but do not sacrifice. As I have
previously stated, both the motive and manner of the sacrifice differ amongst the tribes,
though the rite itself is invariably performed
with great cruelty.

The victims, called "Meriah," must be

bought with a price. This condition is essential. They may be of any age, sex or caste, but adults are most esteemed as being the most costly and, therefore, the most acceptable to the deity. They are sometimes purchased from their parents or relations, when these have fallen into poverty, or in seasons of famine ; but they are often stolen from the plains by professed kidnappers. In some cases Meriah women are allowed to live until they have had children to Khond fathers, which children are reared for sacrifice, but are not put to death in the village where they are born, but exchanged for children of a similar birth from another village. They are always well treated. The price of a victim is rarely paid in money, almost universally in kind, and varies from ten to sixty articles. Cattle, pigs, or goats, brass vessels or ornaments are the chief medium of barter. The sacrifice must be celebrated in public before the assembled people.

Persons are also purchased by the Khonds, or procured by them for adoption into their families, as helps in household affairs, and in the labours of cultivation. These are called "Possiapoes," adopted children, and are usually obtained when young. They often marry into the family of their protector, and in the course of time merge into, and are lost in the general mass of inhabitants.

I may here quote the following interesting portions of a Report by Mr. Russell, relating to human sacrifices, and dated 11th May, 1837.

"In the 'Maliahs' (hill tracts) of Goomsur, the sacrifice is offered annually to 'Tada Penoo,' the earth god under the effigy of a peacock, with the view of propitiating the deity to grant favourable crops. The 'Zani,' or priest, who may be of any caste, officiates at the sacrifice, but he performs the 'Pooga,' (offering of flowers, incense, &c.) to the idol, through the medium of the 'Zoomba,' who must be a Khond boy under seven years of age, and who is fed and clothed at the public expense, eats alone, and is subjected to no act deemed impure.

"For a month prior to the sacrifice, there is much feasting, intoxication, and dancing round the 'Meriah,' (victim) who is adorned with garlands, &c., and on the day before the performance of the barbarous rite, is stupified with toddy, and is made to sit, or is bound at the bottom of a post, bearing the effigy above described. The assembled multitude then dance round to music, and addressing the earth say, ' O God, we offer this sacrifice to you; give us good crops, seasons, and health;' after which they address the victim. ' We bought you with a price, and did not seize you; now we sacrifice you according to custom, and no sin rests with us.'

" On the following day, the victim being again intoxicated, and anointed with oil, each individual present touches the anointed part, and wipes the oil on his own head. All then march in procession round the village and its boundaries, preceded by music, bearing the victim in their arms. On returning to the post, which is always placed near the village idol called ' Zacari Penoo,' represented by three stones, a hog is killed in sacrifice, and the blood being allowed to flow into a pit prepared for the purpose, the victim who has been previously made senseless from intoxication, is seized and thrown in, and his face pressed down till he is suffocated in the bloody mire. The Zani then cuts a piece of flesh from the body, and buries it near the village idol, as an offering to the earth. All the people then follow his example, but carry the bloody prize to their own villages, where part of the flesh is buried near the village idol, and part on the boundaries of the village. The head of the victim remains unmutilated, and with the bare bones is buried in the bloody pit.

"After this horrid ceremony has been completed, a buffalo calf is brought to the post, and his four feet having been cut off, is left there till the following day. Women, dressed in male attire and armed as men, then drink, dance and sing round the spot, the calf is killed and eaten, and the Zani

dismissed with a present of rice, and a hog
or calf. Of the many ways in which the
unhappy victim is destroyed, that just
described is perhaps the least cruel, as in
some places the flesh is cut off while the
unfortunate creature is still alive."

This, then, was all that we knew in May,
1837, of the sacrifice of human beings
among the Khond tribes of the Hill tracts
of Orissa. A few extracts from the Report
above quoted, as to the dangers attending
the attempt to abolish this barbarous practice, will not be out of place.

" No one is more anxious for the discon-
tinuance of this barbarous practice than I
am, but I am strongly impressed with the
belief that it can be accomplished only by
slow and gradual means. We must not
allow the cruelty of the practice to blind us
to the consequences of too rash a zeal in

our endeavours to suppress it. The superstition of ages cannot be eradicated in a day, the people with whom we have to deal have become known to us only within the last few months, and our intercourse has been confined to a very small portion of a vast population, among the greater part of whom the same rites prevail, and of whose country and language we may be said to know almost nothing. Any measure of coercion would arouse the jealousy of a whole race, possessing the strongest feeling of clanship, and whatever their ordinary dissensions, likely to make common cause in support of their common religion. The 'Bissois,' the only people who could possibly be expected to second our views, have only a few peons in whom they could rely on such an occasion. The great mass of their subjects are Khonds, their influence

D

is the moral effect of habit, not of physical power; and men thus situated cannot be expected to aid in the compulsory abolition of a custom which all the surrounding tribes hold sacred. Are the government prepared to engage in an undertaking, which, to be effectual, must lead to the permanent occupation of an immense territory, and involve us in a war with people with whom we have now no connection, and no cause for quarrel, in a climate inimical to the constitution of strangers, and at an expense which no human foresight can calculate?

"From all I have seen of them, I feel convinced that no system of coercion can succeed. Our aim should be to improve to the utmost our intercourse with the tribes nearest to us, with a view to civilize and enlighten them, and so reclaim them from the savage practice, using our moral influence rather than our power. The position we now hold in Goomsur is favourable to the purpose, and it probably is so in some places beyond the frontier also."

In a Minute of consultation of a subsequent date, the Hon. Mr. Russell writes,

" Captain Campbell has acquired a knowledge of the country and people of the Hill tracts in the Ganjam district, under circumstances never likely to occur again, and his local experience and personal influence with the different Hill chieftains, give him an advantage over any other person who could be appointed to the situation of Principal Assistant to the Commissioner."

I have made these quotations to shew the small extent, at this period, of our knowledge regarding both the people and the countries where human sacrifices prevailed; and further to prove the difficulties and dangers which beset the question, of the measures best adapted for the suppression of these revolting ceremonies. It may also be gathered from the extracts what amount of personal influence I was likely to bring to bear upon the minds of the Khonds from my knowledge and experience acquired during the war, immediately subsequent to which it pleased the Government to appoint me to the revenue and magisterial charge of Goomsur, Sooradah, Boodaguddah, Daracota and Aska, with special charge over the Khond inhabitants of these countries.

CHAPTER III.

IN December, 1837, I ascended the
Khond Hills, escorted by a few " Irregulars," raised by myself from the inhabitants
of the village skirting the mountain range.
These recruits were bold and hardy fellows,
inured to the climate, and from their youth
upwards accustomed to bear arms. Several
of them had earned distinctive titles, bestowed by their rajahs for deeds of gallau-
try. For instance, one was called " Joogar
Singh," which means " Lion in War ;" an-

other "Runnah Singh," or "Strong in
battle;" another "Poki Singh," "Swifter
than a Lion," and so forth.

Amongst these men, a few possessed a
slight colloquial knowledge of the Khond
dialect, and were of great value to me.

I called to my councils the intrepid old
chief, Sam Bissoi of Hodzagur, who had
been raised for his invaluable services during the campaign to the dignity of chief of
the Khonds of Goomsur, by the title of
"Buhadur Bukhshi," with whom I was
well acquainted, and who had been my
companion during the war in many a
harassing "dour" and skirmish; and having fully explained my views, the plan of
procedure, and the part I expected him to
perform—into which he most heartily entered—I summoned all the chiefs of villages and "Mootas" of the Goomsur

"Maliahs," (mountains,) to assemble with
their "Digalos" at Oodiagerry, the fort of
the late rajah.

These men had all received the turban of
investiture to office from my hands, at the
conclusion of the war, and consequently
knew me well, and at the time appointed
nearly all attended, to the number of about
three hundred, accompanied by so many of
their Khond followers, attracted by curiosity, that there could not have been fewer
than three thousand men present.

I sat under the shade of a tree, the
Khond chiefs ranged in a semicircle in front,
seated on the ground, and the others collected in groups around us. Through Sam
Bissoi and another Ooryah chief of some
influence, named Punda Naik, I explained
to the assembly the horror with which we
viewed the rite of human sacrifice. " In

no part of our dominions did it exist, and now that they were British subjects they too must abandon it. The subjects of the state, whether Khond or Ooryah, are the children of the state, and wherever the life of one of her children was taken, then a life assuredly would be required. Was it not their own law—life for life. Ages past, we too sacrificed human beings, but we were then fools and ignorant, now we know better, and desire to give the same wisdom to our subjects, that they may learn the uselessness and sin of human sacrifices, may live at peace with each other, and be prosperous. The inhabitants of the plains, and even several of the neighbouring Khond tribes do not sacrifice human beings, and where are there stronger men or finer crops?"

Every argument I could think of, likely

to make an impression on such minds, was used, and finally I requested that they would discuss the question among themselves, and let me know the result of their deliberation. The assembly then broke up, and I waited their reply in great anxiety, for a compromise had been proposed to me, of permitting one sacrifice annually for the whole of the Khonds of Goomsur. This proposal was at once sternly rejected.

The assembly again met, and after some preliminaries, five or six of the oldest and most influential of the Khond chiefs came forward to express the sentiments of the majority of the meeting, which they did with great self-possession and remarkable fluency, to the following purport :

" We have always sacrificed human beings. Our fathers handed down the custom to us. They thought no wrong, nor did we; on the contrary we felt we were doing what was right. We were then the subjects of the Rajah of Goomsur, now we are the subjects of the Great Government, whose orders we must obey. If the earth refuses its produce, or disease destroys us, it is not our fault, we will abandon the sacrifice, and will, if permitted, like the inhabitants of the plains, sacrifice animals."

It would be tedious to relate all that passed, and the long and exciting discussions which ensued, but in the end the assembly was dismissed with orders to meet again on a certain day, bringing with them all the victims intended for sacrifice. The result was most gratifying, and far beyond my most sanguine hopes. At the appointed time, nearly one hundred human beings, male and female, intended for sa-crifice were delivered to me.

The assembly was again harangued by myself as on the first day, and subsequently the people were addressed by several influential Khond speakers, who impressed upon them the necessity of obedience to the orders of the State.

The chiefs then took an oath peculiar to themselves. Seated on tiger skins, they held in their hands a little earth, rice and water, repeating as follows :

" May the earth refuse its produce, rice choke me, water drown me, and tiger devour me and my children, if I break the oath which I now take for myself and my people to abstain for ever from the sacrifice of human beings."

My sword was then passed round from chief to chief, as a mark of submission on their part, and of protection on mine. Presents were distributed, and I then dissolved my second Khond Assembly, and they returned to their homes.

Some chiefs of the more distant villages had failed to bring their Meriahs, but seeing how their fellow chieftains had acted, soon followed their example; and thus one hundred and five Meriahs were, in less than one month's operations, rescued from a cruel death. They were of different ages. Many were restored to their relations on the plains, some were eagerly sought after for adoption by handicraftsmen, and others in the low country. The civil and military officers took charge of a few, and I had twelve instructed as domestic servants, and to be employed as interpreters in our future intercourse with the Khonds.

For four years I continued to watch over
the Khonds of Goomsur, visiting them
once, sometimes twice, every year, and
during these visits settling all their important affairs. From their most serious dif-
ferences, even blood feuds down to the
simplest family quarrels, in which the fair
sex bore a prominent part, I was their
arbitrator; and by giving them at all times
free access to me, and joining in their
hunting parties, I acquired their confidence
in no slight degree, and was enabled to exercise the influence thus obtained for the
attainment of the benevolent objects of the
Government.

Many visited me at my dwelling on
the plains, such was the confidence in-
spired by the facility which had been
afforded them for attending fairs in the
low country, where they were carefully

protected, and soon became expert bar-
gainers.

I instituted a strict search after kidnappers, and apprehended three notorious
offenders, who were brought to trial and
imprisoned.

I recommended the construction of a
road through the heart of the Khond
country, as the first great step towards the
civilization of the inhabitants, and I urged,
with all the force I could use, the necessity
of extending operations for the suppression
of the Meriah rite, into the neighbouring
principalities of Boad and Chinna Kimedy.

My health had suffered much from personal exposure in these unhealthy regions;
where a tree, or a straw heap was very
frequently my only shelter at night—
nothing to be complained of on service in
the field, but far from agreeable in the

ordinary routine of a peaceful duty ; but I was well repaid by the peace and repose which universally prevailed in the countries under my charge, and in the fact that in January, 1842, the Meriah sacrifice was at an end among the Khonds of Goomsur, though I did not pretend to have eradicated all inclination for the rite from the minds of these wild people.

Thus terminated what I may designate as my first campaign, with the special object of conquering the religious prejudices of the wild tribes of Goomsur, and extinguishing their atrocious rite of sacrificing human victims.

I desire in all sincerity to speak with diffidence of my own exertions, and I regret the necessity of such frequent and unavoidable use of the personal pronoun. But I may be allowed warmly to rejoice over the results of these five years of labour. The chieftains and their tribes were my attached friends. A commencement of civilization had been made, more than one hundred victims saved from a violent and bloody death, and the public performance of the Meriah sacrifice entirely suppressed amongst the Hill Tribes of Goomsur.

CHAPTER IV.

EARLY in the year 1842 I took leave of
my Khond subjects, and joined my regiment proceeding on service to China.

Captain Macpherson was then appointed
to the charge of the Goomsur Khonds, he
having previously with a large establishment—a doctor, a company of soldiers, and
five elephants, provided by Government to
carry his tents—proceeded into the Khond
country of Soorada, where female infanti-

E

cide was known to prevail. Unused to the feverish climate of these mountains, he returned after an absence of about twenty-five days, prostrated with fever, and his escort and followers totally disorganised from the same cause.

In 1843 and 1844 he passed a few days in each year in the Goomsur Khond country, but did not go far into the interior, nor indeed was there any necessity for his doing so, for the Khonds had given up the Meriah sacrifice, though they were clamorous, (as when I had left them) that their neighbours of Boad and Chinna Kimedy should also be compelled to relinquish the rite. In these countries the abominable Meriah was openly performed, and in several instances the flesh of the sacrifice, brought from thence to their fields by the Khonds of Goomsur, was a sore trial to such as were sincerely desirous of adhering to their pledge.

Most unhappily for himself and the country under his charge, Captain Macpherson conceived a prejudice against the bold and independant chief, Sam Bissoi, and in an evil hour the Government was persuaded to sanction the banishment of this chief and several of his family. His dignities were taken from him, and also his estate and country, and in his place Ootan Sing Dulbera, priest of Tentulgur, was set up. Captain Macpherson restored to this man with much pomp, an idol formerly in the Dulbera's keeping.

About the middle of 1844, Captain Macpherson went to Calcutta. His assistant, Mr. Cadenhead, visiting the Khond country a few months after Sam Bissoi's expulsion, found the new chief, Ootan Sing of

Tentulgur, insulted and derided, without
authority or power, and the Khonds banded
together under a son of Sam Bissoi's, who
had been thought too insignificant to be
removed, calling for the restoration of their
old chief, and threatening to revert to their
ancient sacrifice, unless their neighbours of
Boad and Chinna Kimedy were coerced
like themselves.

The removal of Sam Bissoi, one of the
oldest and most influential of all the Ooryah
chiefs, had been a fatal mistake, and had
had the most injurious effects on the chieftains of the same class in Boad. It in-
spired the resolute with a spirit of opposition, and the timid fled into concealment.
Captain Macpherson soon discovered his
error, for he reports that the new chief,
Ootan Sing, had so disgusted all by his
avarice, his want of courage, and his bad

faith, that he was compelled to contemplate his removal.

Such was the condition of the Khond "Maliahs" of Goomsur in 1845.

At this time the Agency for the Suppression of Human Sacrifice was remodelled, and extended powers conferred upon the agent, Captain Macpherson, who with three European assistants, a large native establishment, and thirteen elephants took the field in Boad early in 1846.

"He found," as he states, "the Boad tribes more prepared than he had ventured to hope to adopt the required changes. Every tribe was pledged by its representatives after the manner of the Goomsur tribes, to relinquish the Meriah rite, and then the holders of victims bringing them with emulous haste, in seven days about one hundred and seventy were delivered to him."

But, alas! this promising commencement was of short duration, for a few days later the agent's camp was surrounded by a mob of Khonds, who compelled him to restore to them the victims that one week before they were said to have brought in with " emulous haste."

The same night the agent struck his camp, and marched towards Goomsur carrying the Rajah of Boad with him; but the Khonds gaining courage from this apparent flight, pursued the agent, and being joined by some of the Goomsur tribes, demanded the freedom of the Boad Rajah, which was yielded them, and the retreat continued till the arrival of reinforcements from the plains, when the Khonds were driven away.

This was a lamentable beginning of the new agency from which so much had been expected. The Khonds were triumphant, the God of Victory, "Manicksoro," had conquered, and the bloody sacrifice of the Meriah was secure.

The gross corruption and extortion practised by the principal native servants of the agent's establishment towards the people of Boad, whose minds were thereby alienated and alarmed, were, I am satisfied, the moving causes of this sudden revulsion of feeling evinced by the Khonds, from the disposition to bring in their Meriahs, to the armed resolution with which they demanded their restoration.

The rainy season was now at hand, when the climate of the hills has a fatal effect on the health of both Europeans and natives of the plains. The agent was compelled to

quit the Khond " Maliahs," and return to
the low country to prepare for the operations of the next season, when it was hoped
he would recover both the prestige he had
lost, and the wretched victims he had delivered over to the exasperated Khonds.

During the rainy season, the Ooryah and
Khond chiefs of Boad and Chokapaud, (a
hill valley of Goomsur) were not idle, for
they assembled a considerable number of
matchlock men, many of them from Goomsur, led by Chokro Bissoi, the nephew of
Dora Bissoi, formerly chief of the Goomsur
Khonds, and who was in this emergency
brought from the neighbouring principality
of Ungool.

In November, 1846, Captain Macpherson again ascended into the Khond country of Boad, with a considerable force. He
found almost every village deserted on his

approach, and the inhabitants concealed in the recesses of their jungles, to which, in many instances, they had conveyed their grain and valuables. The deserted villages were burned, and the jungle strongholds searched for by the troops, who, on several occasions, were stoutly opposed; but there were no symptoms of submission, though the principal positions were in full military possession.

At this time, seeing that his matchlock-men could not contend successfully with the sepoys, Chokro Bissoi devised and skil-fully executed a descent into the plains of Goomsur, where he and his followers com-menced plundering and burning villages in retaliation of and after the example set them in Boad.

This lamentable state of affairs both in the Hill tracts of Boad and in the plains of

Goomsur, continued till March 1847, when Major-General Dyce, in command of the northern division of the Madras army, was empowered to take upon himself complete political authority in the whole of the territory under the control of the agent in the Hill tracts of Orissa, and was instructed to establish the most direct intercourse with the chiefs of the Hill tribes, and to give the people in opposition to our Government a clear and correct view of the benevolent intentions entertained towards them.

Major-General Dyce reported on the 20th of March, "that he wished to give all the assistance in his power to Captain Macpherson to give effect to his measures for the restoration of tranquillity, but no change had taken place in the aspect of affairs, and he had come to the conclusion after communicating with many influential persons, and from actual observation, that tranquillity would not be restored under the present agency, owing to the extreme hatred manifested throughout these districts against Captain Macpherson and his establishment—the result as is generally stated of the oppressive conduct of the Agency towards the inhabitants of these " Mootas," and above all the harsh and cruel measures resorted to, whenever it has been necessary to display the power, as it is termed, of the Government against any of these ignorant and deluded people."

I am very unwilling to dwell upon this painful portion of the measures pursued for the suppression of the Meriah sacrifice in Boad, suffice it to say, the policy pursued by General Dyce was most successful. The removal of Captain Macpherson and his establishment at once put an end to the opposition to Government, tranquillity was restored, and nothing remained but the embers of the disturbance kept alive by Chokro Bissoi, the leader of the matchlock men, whose opposition in Boad, and atrocities in the plains of Goomsur, placed him beyond the pale of forgiveness.

In the meanwhile I had returned with my regiment from China, where I had received the honour of the third class of the Order of the Bath, and the brevet rank of Lieutenant-Colonel, and was employed in suppressing an insurrection in Golconda, a hill Zumendary to the southward of Vizagapatam, which happily was overcome; but the climate was fatal to several of my officers and men, and I also suffered so severely from fever that I was compelled to go to sea and Ceylon for the recovery of my health.

In January, 1847, the Government of India being dissatisfied with and alarmed at the results of the policy pursued by Captain Macpherson, and contemplating his removal from the Khond Agency, requested the most noble the Marquis of Tweedale, the Governor and Commander-in-Chief of the Madras Presidency, to recommend an officer to supersede him. 1 was named, and was ordered to proceed to the scene of the disturbances without delay, and I left Madras about the time that General Dyce had arrived in Goomsur.

I mention this fact to show that the supercession of Captain Macpherson was the premeditated act of the Supreme Government, and that this intention was merely confirmed not originated by General Dyce's most faithful reports of the miserable state in which he found both

Boad and Goomsur. Indeed, months
before, on the 17th of May, 1846, the
Secretary to the Government of India wrote
to Captain Macpherson :—

" I am directed to express the regret of
His Honour in Council that your operations
for the suppression of human sacrifice
among the Khonds have, in this first season
of your proceedings, been attended with
untoward circumstances, not anticipated by
the Government. It was a very serious
error, when engaging in hostilities attended
with lamentable consequences, and you
found it necessary to call for military support, to imagine that Government would
be satisfied to receive the only accounts
which it possessed of the position in which
you were placed from common rumour or
newspaper reports."

In May, 1847, I received charge of the

Agency for the Suppression of Human Sacrifice and Female Infanticide in the Hill Tracts of Orissa.

The corrupt practices of the native establishment of the late Agency made it impossible to employ any of them, and I had new instruments to form, a work of great difficulty.

Early in November of the same year, accompanied by the now broken down and disheartened old chief, Sam Bissoi, who had been recalled from banishment, I ascended the ghats into the Goomsur Khond country, and it was affecting to see the reverence with which the people received their old "Abba," as they called him, as he passed them on his way to Hodghogur, his paternal property.

From Goomsur I marched into Boad, and placed myself in communication with the Rajah and his principal officers, and those Khond chiefs whose confidence in us had been restored by the publication of proclamations extensively circulated, announcing the removal of the late Agency and clearly explaining the views of Government, and the principles on which I intended to carry them out.

We had not proceeded far in our preliminary measures, when I was unexpectedly ordered to to take command of a military expedition into Ungool, a Hill principality bordering on that of Boad, on the north side of the Mahanuddi river: the Supreme Government having determined to coerce the Rajah, who was refractory, and had committed several atrocities on villagers, subjects of a neighbouring principality, and scornfully refused to give any redress. I had political charge as well as military command of the expedition, which in two months was brought to a successful termination, by the dispersion of the troops of the Rajah, the destruction of his forts, and the capture of the Rajah himself, together with his principal advisers. For these services, I received the thanks of the Governor-General of India in Council.

During my absence in Ungool, my assistant, Captain Macviccar was placed in charge of Boad and Goomsur, with directions to abstain from all aggressive movements unless absolutely necessary, but to keep the disaffected in check. At this time an attempt was made to sacrifice a young girl, who had been shewn to and accepted by their supposed deity, and the day for sacrifice appointed; but through the energetic measures adopted by Captain Macviccar, the Meriah was rescued, and

F

four Khond chiefs, leaders in the proposed sacrifice, cleverly captured.

On the 19th of February, 1848, I left Ungool, and marched to Boad with three companies of the 29th regiment, three of the 41st, and a small party of the Ramghur Horse. I found that Chokro Bissoi had obtained a strong hold on the Khonds of Boad by his succesful resistance last season to Captain Macpherson, and his promising to procure for them the uninterrupted performance of the Meriah sacrifice. This bold promise was precisely adapted to gain the devotion of the Khonds, and the struggle about to ensue was to settle the point whether the Government could, or could not enforce its will of putting a stop to the immolation of human beings. Hitherto the Khonds of Boad had been triumphant, and the tokens of success,

one hundred and forty of the victims, unhappily extorted from Captain Macpherson,
were still in their power.

I made a careful distribution of the little
force at my disposal, strictly prohibiting
offensive operations or the slightest injury
of any kind to person or property. Gradually the deserted villages were reoccupied,
and when at last the leading chieftains ap-
proached, matters were ripe for the discussion of the great question which brought
us there.

Long and tedious councils were held,
and every argument considered suitable to persuade them to desist from an
abhorrent rite was applied and enforced ;
but it must be admitted that the determination I unmistakeably manifested, the
plain and forcible exposition of the views of
Government, and the kind reception the

chiefs experienced from me, produced the most effect.

It would be tiresome to recount the circuitous routes we journeyed over; districts unheard of by Europeans were traversed, and more gloomy, pestilential regions are rarely seen; but it was of the first importance that the work in Boad should be a thorough one, and it was essential to satisfy those chiefs who had made their submission that it was no partial business, and that what had been exacted from them would be exacted from all.

The operations in Boad were protracted to an unusually late period in May. At this time of the year, the rank grass and underwood in the jungles is set fire to, in anticipation of the rains in June, and the heat from the sun and dense hot smoke from the fires burning on every hill, make the climate almost unbearable.

Severe cases of fever were alarmingly prevalent amongst all classes, many of whom were sent from time to time to the low country, where, I grieve to say, two of the officers died. Cheered, however, by each day's successful work, it was impossible to stop ; and I had the satisfaction of reporting that with two exceptions every influential man in Boad had completely submitted to the will of the Government, and pledged himself, by swearing in the most solemn manner, henceforth to abstain from the Meriah sacrifice ; and in token of their submission and obedience they delivered two hundred and thirty-five Meriah victims, including those surrendered by Captain Macpherson, with the exception of three who had been sacrificed. One of

the modes of sacrifice in Boad is as follows :—

Three days previous to immolation there
is great feasting, rioting, and dancing, and
the most gross and brutal licentiousness.
On the fourth day the Meriah is taken
round the village in procession to each door,
when some pluck hair from his head, and
others solicit a drop of spittle, with which
they anoint their own heads. Afterwards the
victim is drugged, and then taken to the
place of sacrifice, his head and neck being
introduced into the reft of a strong bamboo
split in two, the ends of which are secured
and held by the sacrificers. The presiding
priest then advances, and with an axe
breaks the joints of the legs and arms; the
surrounding mob then strip off the flesh
from the bones with their knives, and each
man having secured a piece, carries the

quivering and bloody morsel to his fields, and there buries it.

The rebel Chokro Bissoi after some trifling resistance, was fairly hunted out of the country, bitterly upbraiding the Khonds with having deserted him, and I had the satisfaction of reporting to the Government that tranquillity had been restored to Boad and Goomsur.

The rainy season was passed in the low country, recruiting our health and preparing for operations for the suppression of the Meriah sacrifice in Chinna Kimedy.

72

CHAPTER V.

CHINNA KIMEDY is a principality a little
to the south and west of Goomsur, having
about one hundred and twenty villages on
the plains, which are fertile. The inhabitants are for the most part Ooryahs, who
have frequently suffered from the incursions
of the adjoining mountaineers, (Khonds)

whose savage valour generally obtained for them an easy victory—while in case of a reverse, their fastnesses received them and their impenetrable jungles afforded a secure retreat.

The late Rajah was accused of tyrannical conduct by the Khond tribes, who professed allegiance to him, and they invaded and devastated the low country, carrying the Rajah and his three sons captives to their mountains. After some time, the old man was ransomed for a considerable sum, and his son, the present Rajah, released, because he was supposed to be at enmity with his father. From this little sketch, it will be apparent that the low country Rajahs are most unwilling to risk a collision with the Hill tribes, and this was an important fact to be borne in mind in our attempts to suppress human sacrifice. There must necessarily be a good understanding between the chiefs and us, but no such overt act as might tend to infuriate the Khonds against their Rajahs, as aiders and abettors in extirpating their long cherished rite.

The Khond "Maliahs" of Chinna Kimedy comprise a portion of the chain of mountains in continuation of those of Boad and Goomsur, to both of which it adjoins. The inhabitants are essentially of the same stock, and their tribal divisions very similar. The Khond chiefs of villages and "Mootas" are termed "Maji," instead of "Mulliko" as in Goomsur, or "Khonro" as in Boad, and the chiefs of districts "Patur" instead of "Bissoi."

The sacrifice in Chinna Kimedy is not offered to the earth alone as in Goomsur and Boad, but to a number of deities,

whose power is essential to life and happiness; of these " Manicksoro," god of war,
" Boro Penoo," the great god, " Zara
Penoo," the sun god, hold the chief place.
The time of sacrifice is a time of unmitigated
revelry, in which the women share. In
some districts the victim, after certain
ceremonies, is flung violently to the ground
and held or bound down while the flesh is
cut off piece-meal. The shreds thus procured are afterwards buried in their fields.
Another mode of sacrifice I will describe
further on.

Several of the most inaccessible tribes
have never acknowledged the authority of
the Rajah, and generally the sacrificing
Khonds of Chinna Kimedy do not visit the
plains to attend the fairs, as do those of
Goomsur and Bood, but dispose of their
turmeric, their sole article of barter, for

salt, cloth, or brass vessels, to traders from
the plains, who are also very frequently
professed kidnappers.

Considering the character given of the
people, it was by no means improbable that
resistance might be attempted, and from
our ignorance of them and of their country,
the enterprise was an arduous one, and it
was necessary to provide for all contin-
gencies.

Nothing but the sternest necessity would
ever cause me in this good work to use
force, but I felt satisfied that the resolute
expression of the will of Government, and
the assumption of a determined attitude,
which would declare more plainly than
words the fruitlessness of all attempts at
opposition, was at once the most merciful
and most effectual way of accomplishing
our object.

The Governor-General of India in Council having expressed every confidence in my experience and judgment, authorised me to prosecute my measures in such manner as might appear to me expedient. Thus trusted, and my policy supported by the Most Noble the Marquis of Dalhousie, I entered with confidence on my mission.

Previously, however, to commencing my difficult task in Chinna Kimedy, I paid a visit to the hill country or "Maliahs" of Soorada, where female infanticide largely prevails. In about thirty villages, two hundred and thirty-one boys were counted under ten years of age, and only twenty females under that age, and even the few rescued Meriah girls who had been given in marriage to Khonds of the infanticidal tribes, were found to have destroyed their female offspring, or to have suffered them to die in obedience to their husbands' commands.

As a sample of the many fables which are common as to the origin of female infanticide, I give the following.

In ancient times there was a man called "Denko Mullico," who had four sons. Of these four brothers, the three eldest begat eight sons each, and the youngest, two daughters, who could get no husbands, and in consequence became connected with certain of their cousins. This sad circumstance induced the brothers, whose sons were not guilty, to deprive the brother, whose sons had contaminated their female cousins, of all his property. On this, the two guilty females drowned themselves in a tank called "Reda bondo." Afterwards, the elder brothers condoled with the disgraced younger brother, and concluding

that their alienation from, and contention
with him, was occasioned by his female
issue, they then determined that thence-
forward their female issue should be destroyed, and solemnised this determination
by invoking their deities "Poboodi" and
"Boropenoo;" and since that time the
practice of female infanticide has been maintained.

The Khonds here say that in obedience
to orders to discontinue the custom, they
had tried to do so, but that, nevertheless,
their female children died, which they attribute to having violated the solemn oath of
their ancestors.

This custom, however, does not in reality
spring from religious feeling, but is practised as a matter of convenience. The
Khonds of these tribes, when they marry,
give an equivalent to the wife's father for

her, which the father is obliged to repay to
the husband should she desert him for another man, from whom the father can then
claim the equivalent. This gives rise to
endless difficulties and broils of frequent
occurrence, which they think to avoid by
marrying women from distant places, for
whom they give a much smaller sum than
for wives of their own tribe. Moreover, they
profess to consider it degrading to give
their daughters in marriage to men of their
own tribe, and that it becomes their own
manliness to marry only the daughters of
a distant country.

The remedy for this inhuman and unna-
tural crime is a perplexing and difficult
question. The people pleaded poverty, and
the influence of long transmitted tradition
as their justification. I endeavoured by
every means in my power, to convince

them of the heinous crime of depriving a
child of life because it was a female, and I
declared that if they persisted in doing so,
it would be considered as a most serious
offence and treated accordingly.

I tried to remove from their minds the
prejudice against marrying females of their
own community, and promised them wives
from the rescued Meriahs, whom I hoped
would, when in greater numbers, exercise a
favourable influence, and be a check on the
other inhabitants. The assembled chiefs
then signed an agreement henceforward to
rear their female offspring. It was the
best remedy I could devise, and I left an
intelligent native officer to watch over them.

The manner in which these infanticidal
tribes of Soorada pay homage to a superior
is very remarkable, and to a stranger
alarming. They rush into the camp in a

G

compact phalanx of from sixty to two hundred men, uttering shrill cries, brandishing their battle-axes, and circling at a run, they advance and retire in imitation of a fight, and at last charge straight at the dignitary ready to receive them, to whom they present their offering of rice, a few addled eggs, and a kid. They then seat themselves on the ground, with the chiefs and " Majis " in front, and business commences.

When preferring a complaint, a Khond or Panoo will throw himself on his face on the ground, with hands joined, and a bunch of straw or grass in his mouth; and I have more than once found myself in danger of a fall by the violent shying of my horse, at the sudden appearance of three or four of these complainants throwing themselves on the ground before him.

I was hurried away from my labours among the infanticidal tribes in Soorada by intelligence which reached me of a general sacrifice of Meriahs, resolved on by the Khonds of Chinna Kimedy, rather than that they should fall into my hands. I hastened onwards, and my sudden, though not altogether unexpected appearance, stayed the murderous proceeding.

I was fully alive to the necessity of proceeding with the extremest caution on my first introduction to a wild and warlike race of men, who, of necessity, were prejudiced against me, as a subverter of their ancient and much loved rite. I was sensible that any false or hasty step might plunge me into war with the whole of these tribes, and horrible indeed would have been a warfare in these dense forests, and almost unknown mountains, where the climate was

not the least deadly foe we should have had
to contend against.

In the outset, I had the good fortune to
conciliate and gain the confidence of Rajah
Adikund Deo, of Chinna Kimedy, and of
his tributary Rognat Deo, Tat Rajah of
Guddapore, and their subordinate chiefs.
This was a great step, for without their aid
and co-operation I could scarcely have
hoped to accomplish the object in view,
save by recourse to measures of severity
painful even to contemplate.

I purposely avoided placing these rajahs
at any time in antagonism with their hill
subjects. I never allowed them to appear
on the scene when the slightest appearance
of coercion was needful, but confined all
such acts exclusively to my own establishment; though following my invariable
course of procedure, I employed an inter-

mediate cutchery agency as little as possible, and placed myself at once in direct communication with all classes.

From the very first, I openly, and in the most plain and intelligible manner, proclaimed the chief design of my appearance among them. Without any disguise or circumlocution, I told them that Government had sent me for the sole and avowed purpose of putting an end for ever to the inhuman and barbarous murders yearly perpetrated by them, and if needful, force the surrender of all the victims held in possession, and destined to die this cruel death. All their other ancient usages, I impressed upon them, would be strictly respected; the Government was anxious to befriend them, and willing to assist them. If any were suffering oppression, redress should be afforded, and justice meted out with an impartial hand, but this Meriah sacrifice, this inhuman practice must at once and for ever be laid aside. This plain speaking was eminently beneficial, there was and could be no mistake in their minds regarding the unalterable resolve of Government, and the presence of my armed escort, added not a little to the weight of my declarations.

The Chinna Kimedy Maliahs are divided into seven districts. The several districts, which are each ruled by an Ooryah chief, or "Patur," are subdivided into "Mootas" and villages, and these are governed respectively by a Khond chief, styled "Maji," as in the Maliahs of Soorada. Between these districts there is but little intercourse, owing to the feuds which are constantly occurring.

In the secondary range of mountains the

villages are far apart, and the valleys,
with very few exceptions, present a poor
and barren appearance, contrasting, in this
respect, most unfavourably with the more
richly cultivated valleys of Boad and Goomsur. Water is less abundant than in the
higher range, and barren and uninviting is
the country in every particular, the eye be-
holding only a succession of mountains,
thickly covered with the ordinary " damur"
tree, and with bamboo. The districts on
the upper range, or table-land, are more
picturesque, and open valleys may there be
seen in a high state of cultivation, and
abundantly watered.

Throughout these mountains, human sacrifice, or female infanticide, prevails, with
the exception of the large and fertile districts of Sarungudda, Chundragerry, and
Deegee, where, happily, though surrounded

by sacrificing and infanticidal tribes, (the same race with themselves,) neither the Meriah nor infanticide is practised.

One of the most common ways of offering the sacrifice in Chinna Kimedy, is to the effigy of an elephant, rudely carved in wood, fixed on the top of a stout post on which it is made to revolve. After the performance of the usual ceremonies, the wretched Meriah is fastened to the proboscis of the elephant, and amidst the shouts and yells of the excited multitude of Khonds, is rapidly whirled round, when, at a given signal by the officiating " Zani," or priest, the crowd rush in, seize the Meriah, and with their knives, cut the flesh off the shrieking victim as long as life remains. He is then cut down, the skeleton burnt, and the horrid orgies are over. In several villages, I counted as many as fourteen effigies of elephants, which had been used in former sacrifices. These I caused to be overthrown by the baggage elephants attached to my camp, in the presence of the assembled Khonds, to shew them that these venerated objects had no power against the living animal, and to remove all vestiges of their bloody superstition.

In the large district of Mahasingi of Chinna Kimedy, one hundred purchased individuals were found, several of whom had marks of irons on their wrists and ankles, shewing that they had been fettered to prevent escape. Only fifty-four of this number were destined for sacrifice, the rest had been bought as serfs, or for adoption ("Possia Poes") either by the Ooryah inhabitants, a considerable and influential body, or by the Khond "Majis." When

I was fully satisfied that no foul play was intended towards these serfs, or "Possia Poes," I ordered their re-delivery, first taking a registry of them, and receiving from their several proprietors the usual security, together with a written agreement, whereby they were bound carefully to preserve these individuals, and to produce them when required.

Daily, and almost hourly, were these wild mountaineers assembled in my camp. I wearied both the Khonds and myself with every argument I could think of to induce them to desist from a practice cruel and guilty in the sight of God and man. I recalled to their minds their own law of "life for a life," and challenged them to gainsay, if they could, its justice when applied to their own practice of slaying their fellow-creatures; and I related at length

how I had marched over Goomsur and
Boad, and had swept away every Meriah
from those countries, utterly abolishing the
revolting rite; how their brethren in these
neighbouring countries had most solemnly
pledged themselves never again to sacrifice
human beings, and how abundantly they
had prospered in house and field since abstaining from the rite. I also very spe-
cially directed their attention to the fertile
districts of Sarungudda and Deegee, where
no human blood is shed to propitiate a
sanguinary god, and where the fields are as
productive as their own.

It would be tiresome to recapitulate further details of our many interviews. I had
not quite all the speaking to myself, for I
invariably called on them to reply whether
my speech was true or false, fair or unfair,
and their general answer was, " It is true,

it is just. Our fathers sacrificed and
taught us to do so. The Great Government has sent a mighty chief to forbid the
practice, and he must be obeyed. Let us
then do as our brothers of Goomsur and
Boad have done, and sacrifice buffaloes,
goats, and pigs, instead of human beings."

After many and long conferences, an
agreement was drawn up, as in Goomsur,
and the document signed by all the principal men present, certain binding Khond
formalities being observed to strengthen
their pledge. It was then delivered to me
by the chiefs, who turned round, and addressing the assembled Khonds, called on
them to be true to the pledge which they
had taken, not only for themselves, but for
all. The chiefs were then invested with
turbans. Presents of small sums of money
and strips of red cloth were distributed,

my tent and its contents inspected with wondering curiosity, and the assembly broke up.

As may very naturally be supposed, when it is considered that this was the first time they had been visited by an European, a considerable degree of reserve was frequently evinced by the people. Groups of men, women, and children, sat gazing on at some distance, fearful to enter the camp. They had heard reports, spread by evil-disposed persons, that I was collecting Meriahs, for the purpose of sacrificing them on the plains to the water deity, because the water had disappeared from a large tank which I had constructed, and that my elephants required, periodically, a certain number of Meriahs to be served to them as food.

No effort was spared to undeceive and

conciliate all ranks, and to prove that our object was single in coming among them, and I am happy to think that the opinion entertained of us in the end was not unfavourable. The strictest discipline was maintained in camp, and in no part of the country did person or property receive the slightest damage.

Two hundred and six Meriah victims were rescued in this our 'first season in the "Maliahs" of Chinna Kimedy, though I doubt not some were hidden from us, or carried to a distant part of the country.

From Chinna Kimedy I proceeded into the Boad Hills, where my assistant, Captain Macviccar, had been travelling for some time. The entire abolition of the rite of human sacrifice which so recently prevailed throughout the Maliahs of Boad, is a subject of sincere congratulation. Not one drop of blood had been shed this year at the shrine of their barbarous superstition, nor the least disposition evinced to break the pledge which they had taken last year. The whole of these hills have been traversed, and the same pleasing results exhibited in every quarter.

It may be profitable to dwell for a little on the causes which have produced these most gratifying effects throughout the Hills of Boad and Goomsur, for it appears to me of the last importance that the grounds upon which the suppression has been effected should not be misunderstood, and there seems great danger of misapprehension here, judging from an article in the " Calcutta Review," a magnificent array of language united to a grievous perversion of facts.

In the Boad country, we ought in the

first place to be most thankful to God whose bountiful harvest so powerfully and mercifully seconded our efforts ; and to Him, too, we owe it that during the year the Khonds enjoyed immunity from all but the most ordinary sickness. Next we may ascribe much of our success to the felt and acknowledged power of the Government to enforce its will, that will having always been unreservedly and ' without the slightest compromise declared to the Khonds, wherever met by myself or my assistant, and proclaimed universally throughout the country.

There was no cautious inquisition as formerly recommended, but the glaring fact was dealt with, as an enormity which the Government neither could nor would suffer longer to exist. I mention this prominently, because the success which has attended our labours in Boad and Chinna Kimedy conclusively demonstrates the advantage of a firmer, bolder, and more decided line of policy than was deemed prudent in the days of our earlier connection with these Hills, and 1 venture to assert that if I had met with the same support in 1838-39 as I have since done, the good work of Meriah suppression would in all human probability have been as far advanced in 1841 as it was in 1849.

It could not rationally have been expected that moral persuasion alone—I do not, however, allude to that of the gospel —would or could with such rapidity convert a race of people shrouded in the grossest darkness from a superstition which for centuries had been rivetting its chains. I should indeed have been astonished if the prosperous results which have

blessed our efforts on the Hills could have
been attributed exclusively to the weight
and influence of the moral reasonings we
adduced.　Such discourses should never
be omitted, and every where and on all
occasions impressively urged; but had we
rested on our arguments alone, I fear we
should have effected little.　Hence, in
assigning motives for abstaining from their
ancient rite, the Khonds rarely make
allusion to the moral persuasion that had
been urged upon them, but lay marked
stress upon the futility of all resistance, and
the necessity of obeying the will of the
Government.

I have not alluded to the great precursor
of civilization—the gospel—not because I
am insensible of its fitness for these wild
tribes, who have no prediliction for Brahmins, but simply because it is not within

the province of the Government of India to
introduce any agency of the kind. I may,
however, express the hope that in due
season these poor savages will be visited by
the teachers of a higher and purer wisdom
than that of man.

In this season, from Chinna Kimedy and
Boad, three hundred and seven Meriahs
have been rescued. About one hundred
and twenty little children have been placed
under the care of the missionaries at Berhampore and Cuttack at the expense of the
Government. The married Meriahs,
together with a number of youths of the
same class, have been settled in villages
and set up as cultivators, others have been
apprenticed to different trades, and a few
are learning gardening; about fourteen
have been placed under the protection of
private individuals, and twenty-five have

H 2

enlisted in my corps of Irregulars. The marriageable females are gradually being married to the Khonds of the infanticidal tribes, and others of suitable position, and are sought after as being the wards of Government, from whom they receive a fitting dowry. For the unmarried females and very young children, an asylum has been formed at Soorada under the superintendence of steady matrons, where the young women are practised in household affairs suited to their station; and from whence, at a proper age, the children are removed to the care of the missionaries for instruction.

The road which I recommended to be made into the Goomsur Khond " Maliahs," by the Coormingia Pass, is in progress. One hundred and eighty-four miles of new routes, never before traversed by Europeans, have been surveyed this season in the Khond country, and I have recommended a road to be opened through the Goomsur and Boad "Maliahs," to Sohunpore on the Mahanuddy, not only as facilitating in a military point of view the communication with Nagpore, but as opening up an easy line of road for the extensive traffic which is carried on by the Brinjaries, who are the chief purchasers of the salt manufactured on the sea-coast of the Ganjam district, and which they dispose of in the interior. The moral effect on the Khonds of a well-frequented road passing through their country would be very great.

Lieutenant Frye, an officer whose acquirements as a linguist were of the first order, laboured very zealously in the acquisition of the Khond language. He adopted the Ooryah alphabet as the best suited to

express the sounds of this new dialect; and
to facilitate the study of it by the Ooryahs
attached to the agency, a vocabulary has
been printed, and the Meriah children at
the mission schools at Berhampore readily
understand and converse with Lieutenant
Frye.

The Khond "Maliahs," always insalu-
brious, were most prejudicial this season to
the health of the whole of the Agency
Establishment.   My assistant, Captain
Macviccar, whose services had been beyond
praise, was prostrated with fever, the consequence of exposure and hard work in these
unhealthy mountains, and in the month
of May, 1849, he was sent to the Cape
of Good Hope for the recovery of his
health.

I struggled hard against disease, but at
length was obliged to yield, and in the

month of October following was ordered to the Cape on medical certificate.

I had again the honour of receiving the thanks of the Governor-General of India in Council, and the expression of the lively satisfaction which His Lordship experienced in learning the full and happy results of my exertions.

Captain Frye was appointed my assistant, and I handed over the charge of the Agency to him, fully instructing him in the principles on which the work for the suppression of the Meriah was to be conducted.

CHAPTER VI.

IN December, 1849, during my absence at the Cape, Captain Frye revisited, but by a different route, the same districts of Chinna Kimedy, which I had previously traversed, and have described in the last chapter.

His labours were most successful. A very large number of the persons brought to him were of the serf, or " Possia " class, and he very properly converted into marriage, the state of concubinage in which many of these young women, with their children, were living. The usual security of the chiefs was taken for the well-being and security of these mothers and their off-spring.

All the families restored and settled by me on a similar footing last season, were shewn to Captain Frye.

In the report of his proceedings, Captain Frye states that a Meriah, once shewn to a Government officer, is considered unfit for sacrifice according to the Khond creed. If this were true, there would obviously have existed no necessity for removing a single destined victim; a simple regis-try would have been sufficient. I had painful experience in 1847, of the fallacy of such an idea; it will be remembered that not only were the Boad Meriahs *shewn* to Captain Macpherson, but actually *delivered*, and in his custody, until violently redemanded, and unhappily redelivered to their Khond owners, and three were cruelly sacrificed ere I could save them. It is very transparent why Captain Macpherson adopted this theory of unfitness for sacrifice after being shewn to an official of Government; but I am at a loss to account for Captain Frye's having revived it, as he brought to the plains nearly two hundred Meriahs, (as he supposed), though many were only "serfs," and subsequently restored. Still he was on the safe side in removing them, until absolutely certain that they incurred no risk, and it afforded very convincing proof of the little weight he attached to the assertion of their no longer being regarded as worthy objects of sacrifice.

This officer devoted himself with un-wearied energy to confirming and enlarging the work I had already so happily commenced, and subsequently fell a victim to fever contracted in these sickly hills of Chinna Kimedy.

I gladly bear testimony. to the great merits of this lamented officer.

Early in October, 1850, Captain Macviccar returned to his post of officiating agent.

He visited the tribes of Upper Goomsur, the scene of my earliest labours, and found the people contented and prosperous.

After no inconsiderable opposition and hesitation on the part of the Khonds, he succeeded in establishing four schools. He passed through Boad, saw the Khond chiefs and their tribes who renewed their pledges, and he bestowed on them tokens

of the favour of Government, no human
blood having been shed in Boad for the
last two years.

In Maji Deso, a country midway between
Boad and Patna, he broke fresh ground,
and found that though these Khonds, in
civilization far outstripped their neighbours
of the Boad and Goomsur hills, still they
sacrificed human beings. The custom was
to purchase victims immediately preceding
the sacrifice which is offered to their
deity, not for the purpose of obtaining
cereal produce, but for general prosperity
and blessings for themselves and families.

The mode of performing the sacrifice
equals, if it does not exceed in cruelty, the
practice of other countries. After the appointed ceremonies, the Meriah is surrounded by the Khonds, who beat him vio-

lently on the head with the heavy metal bangles which they generally wear. If this inhuman smashing does not immediately destroy the victim's life, an end is put to his sufferings by strangulation. Strips of flesh are then cut off the body, and each recipient of the precious treasure carries his portion to the stream which waters his fields, and then suspends it on a pole. The remains of the mangled carcase are buried, and funeral obsequies performed seven days after.

The few Meriahs that were in the district were delivered up, and the chiefs pledged in the usual manner to renounce the Meriah rite.

In Patna, which was afterwards traversed, the Khonds gradually delivered up their Meriahs, and swore never again to offer human sacrifice. They are advanced in civilization, well under subjection to their rajah, and pay taxes.

There was much sickness among the people of this Zumendary, several hundreds came to the camp-hospital, thankfully receiving the medicines offered to them, and the kindness and attention shewn them left on their minds a favourable impression.

In the "Mootas" of Sooah, Toopah, and Goakah, it not unfrequently happens that sacrificing and non-sacrificing Khonds are the inhabitants of the same village. They live in harmony, interrupted only for seven days when a victim is slain, at which time the non-sacrificers remain in perfect retirement, and never pass through the front entrance of their houses when they go to their fields until the seven days are expired, then the funeral ceremonies of the poor victim are performed, and all reunite as before.

From the "Mootas" of Patna he passed on with rapidity to Muddenpore, the residence of Koosung Sing, the Tat Rajah, to whom the "Mootas" of Mohungerry Oorla-doni and Taparunga are subject, and from thence eighty-nine Meriahs were removed, and fourteen Possias registered.

Captain Macviccar thus concludes his Report, "The Meriah sacrifice is in abey-ance, if not abolished. Exchange and barter of Meriahs is almost neutralized by the large number removed from that con-tingency. The country in fact is ours, and it only requires vigorous operations on the sacrificing frontier* to render the rite, as regards Chinna Kimedy, one of the things of the past."

* Of Jeypore, which borders on Chinna Kimedy.

He does not think that the cessation of
human sacrifice implies a change of religion,
as had been supposed. " It is well known
that human sacrifice once prevailed in the
low country, but yielded to the superin-
cumbent weight of foreign authority, which,
whether Mussulman or European, extended to the base of the wild hills in
which it now holds sway. The blood-
thirsty Doorga, the dread personification of
evil, is the deity propitiated by the
Khonds, under infinitely diversified forms
and names, and when the deity is obliged
to accept, as at the "Doorga" sacrifice of
the plains, the blood of beasts, the evil of
human sacrifice is at end, although their
religion has undergone no change. The
test then of abolition is the substitution of
an inferior animal as the victim. This has
taken place in Boad and Goomsur, and to

some extent in Patna, but as yet in few places of Chinna Kimedy. Just because they can procure human flesh from a neighbouring country—" The Khond will surrender his victims, and forbear the rite in his own person ; nay, there may not be a single sacrifice throughout the length and breadth of the particular country, but if there be within reach a place where human blood flows on the altar of this superstition, thither its votary will repair, and so long as a morsel of flesh is buried in the field, the rite remains intact, though the loss of human life may be to some extent diminished."

The operations of the season may be briefly summed up.

The tribes of Boad and Goomsur had stood firm to their pledge of abstention from sacrifice, and unruffled tranquillity prevailed. A step in the path of civilization had been taken by the opening of schools.

The Chinna Kimedy tribes gave as yet no symptoms of relapse, and more victims had been given up.

I wish these gratifying results could have been obtained at a less cost of suffering to the European officers employed.

CHAPTER VII.

RETURN TO MY DUTIES AND PROCEED TO MAHASINGI—
SOME DESCRIPTION OF THIS DISTRICT—GO ON TO BISSUM
CUTTACK—ACCOUNT OF HIS LITTLE KINGDOM AND QUAR-
REL WITH RAYAH OF JEYPORE—RESCUE OF MERIAHS—
RYABIJI—CHUNDERPORE—GODAIRY—LUMBARGAM — AT-
TACK ON MY CAMP—ATTACK REPELLED AND MERIAHS
BROUGHT IN—BUNDARI—JUNNAH SACRIFICES—REVISIT
SOORADAH—INFANTICIDE—FLIGHT OF KHONDS TO MY
CAMP—ACCOUNT OF THE MERIAHS SETTLED IN THE
LOW COUNTRY.

EARLY in October, 1851, I returned to
my post. On the 18th November I ascended the Khond mountains, and passing
through the heart of the Goomsur "Mal-
liahs," from whence the Meriah rite had
been thoroughly extirpated, I entered the

I 2

large district of Mahasingi of Chinna Kimedy. The point of this extensive country
which I first reached was Sarungudda, on
the borders of Boad.

The tradition respecting Mahasingi is,
that in former times it was the residence of
a powerful Rajah, who exercised sway over
the districts of Mahasingi, Barcooma, and
Sarungudda. He died, leaving three sons,
the eldest to rule over Mahasingi, the second, over Barcooma, and the third, and
youngest, over Sarungudda and Kurtolly.
The latter, being a good and just man, and
much esteemed by the Khonds, endeavoured to wean them from the sacrifice of
human beings, but not succeeding, he prepared, with all his family and followers, to
leave them, and had made one march towards the plains, when they, moved with
sorrow at the sight of their departing chief,

and having no love for his brothers, into whose hands they were sure to fall, entreated him to return, which, after much persuasion, he consented to do, on condition of their forsaking human sacrifice. To this they agreed, and bound themselves by the most solemn oaths, which, to this day, they have not broken; and the descendants of the younger brother, Cheytun Patur, and Dawdy Patur, now rule over these non-sacrificing tribes, who are as courageous and as prosperous as their neighbours.

I found that the district of Mahasingi had suffered grievously from long-existing feuds, in consequence of which, much land had become waste and neglected. On some of these lands, I was able to settle eighteen Meriah families, in all, fifty-three persons, and near this settlement, in an island formed by a mountain stream, on the site of the ancient fort of Mahasingi, I built a bungalow. According to popular tradition, the fort had been taken posses- sion of by demons, the island deserted, and the fort allowed to go to decay.

From Mahasingi, I penetrated through an unexplored country to Bissum Cuttack of Jeypore, where I found the Tat Rajah, Nairraindur Deo, in considerable uneasiness respecting the object of my mission, for the proclamation regarding it which I had issued some months previously, had not reached him. He was at feud with his superior, the Rajah of Jeypore, who had, about eighteen years before, on pretence of arrears of tribute, seized and imprisoned his father, who, after six years, died in con- finement. During that time, and the six years following, the Rajah of Jeypore ad-

ministered the affairs of Bissum Cuttack,
keeping Nairraindur Deo, who was then
young, under restraint; but about six
years ago, the population of Bissum Cuttack expelled the Rajah of Jeypore's people,
and brought Nairraindur Deo to his fort,
where they had since maintained him.
Thinking I had come to take part against
him, he had some hesitation in visiting me;
but I soon satisfied him as to my intentions, and confidence being established, he
zealously set about assembling the Khond
chiefs of his country, himself in person
going to those distant villages where any
reluctance was shewn by the inhabitants to
come to me, for he holds the Hill tribes in
complete subjection, and has a following of
about five hundred matchlock men.

In his house, I discovered a youth who
had been purchased by him for sacrifice,

and had undergone all the ceremonies preparatory to his immolation to the god of
battles, "Manicksoro," in the event of a
collision with the troops of the Rajah of
Jeypore; which very nearly occurred, for
taking advantage of my presence, the rajah
dispatched a force to Bissum Cuttack; but
I would permit no hostilities, and the force
sent was not strong enough to effect its
purpose without my' countenance. Nairraindur Deo was quite willing to pay the ·
customary tribute to his superior, the Rajah
of Jeypore, but he demanded a settlement
of accounts for the twelve years the Rajah
had administered the revenue of Bissum
Cuttack.

I saw a very large proportion of the inhabitants of this hill Zumendari, and of the
adjoining " Moota" of Doorgi, and I learnt
with much satisfaction, from concurrent

testimony, that with the exception of two small " Mootas," Ambadola and Kunkabody, bordering on Chinna Kimedy, the Meriah sacrifice had ceased for more than two generations, though some of the villages still participated in the cruel rite, by procuring flesh of Meriahs from the neighbouring district of Ryabiji. This flesh, to be efficacious in securing the fertility of their fields, must be deposited in the ground before sunset on the day of the sacrifice, and to ensure this, instances are related of pieces of human flesh having been conveyed, by relays of men, an incredible distance in a few hours.

From the two small " Mootas," Ambadola and Kunkabody, four Meriahs were removed; all, ' I believe, that were in their possession.

From Rajah Nairraindur Deo I received

the youth destined by him for sacrifice. The victim, when offered by the Ooryah chief, is called "Junna;" and this sacrifice is performed on important occasions, such as going to battle, building a fort in an important village, and to avert a danger.

I lost no opportunity of impressing upon the inhabitants collectively and individually the heinousness of the crime of human sacrifice, and that those who were present at the sacrifice, and appropriated part of the flesh for their fields, were little less criminal than the actual sacrificers. At the ceremonial of leave-taking, I presented Rajah Nairraindur Deo with a detonating rifle, which pleased him much.

The inhabitants of this district, are, in civilization, far in advance of the Khonds of Boad and Chinna Kimedy. They speak Ooryah, and are dressed more like Ooryahs

than Khonds, and they carry on a considerable traffic with the plains. The country
also, by comparison, appears well cultivated
after the dense jungly tracts which separate
Chinna Kimedy from Jeypore.

On the 17th of December, we left Bissum Cuttack for Ryabiji, in an easterly
direction, through a mass of jungle and
rugged hills wooded to the top. The
country is badly watered, and the only
cultivation is found round the villages,
which are far apart.

In the "Moota" of Ryabiji, the Meriah
prevails to a great extent, and the Khonds
resemble in appearance and character those
of Chinna Kimedy, but the dialect they
spoke was different, and could with difficulty be understood by my Khond interpreters. Here, ignorant of localities, I was
obliged to feel my way cautiously, for at

the commencement of my operations, the
Ooryah chiefs, not fully comprehending
what was expected of them, were of very
little use. Gradually their confidence increased, and eventually sixty-nine Meriahs
were rescued from Ryabiji "Moota."

Here, as in all other places, the same
language was held to the Khonds respecting the Meriah rite, and all who had
brought in Meriahs, and the chiefs and
principal men of the several villages, signed
the usual pledge to abstain for ever from
the abominable sacrifice.

From Ryabiji to the "Moota" of Chunderpore, our course was to the north and east,
the country being of the same inhospitable
character, affording no supplies of any
kind. There my escort of sepoys became
so disheartened and prostrated by sickness,
both officers and men, that I was obliged

to send them to the plains, retaining only a few of the most hardy of the men; but they too, and my establishment generally, soon gave way, and provisions becoming scarce, I found it necessary to push for the more open country of Godairy.

At Godairy, a large Ooryah village, on the banks of the Bangsadara river, the country is well cultivated, and has a mixed population of Khonds and Sourahs. A considerable traffic in rice and other grains, and timber for building purposes is carried on with the plains. The Khonds, comparatively a civilised race, after some little evasion and procrastination, delivered up their Meriahs to the number of thirteen, and readily entered into the usual agreement to abandon the rite of human sacrifice for ever.

Here I commenced the erection of a

bungalow of three rooms. It was built on posts of about eighteen feet high, with walls of planks, and a thatched roof, after the fashion of the Khond houses, to which was added an open verandah all round, of six feet high. It was intended as a rest house, and as a mark to the Khonds that our visits were not temporary merely, but that we might be among them at any time.

At this place I first came in contact with the Sourah race. They are of a fairer complexion, and their features resembling the Gentoos of the plains, have a better expression than those of the Khonds. They speak a different dialect, they are less dissipated in their habits, and consequently more athletic in their persons, which they adorn with beads and bangles, more common to females than to men. Their arms are the battle-axe, bow and arrow, though a few have matchlocks. They are professed thieves and plunderers, and are the terror of the inhabitants of the plains. Even the Khonds, so ready to fight among themselves, would rather avoid than seek a quarrel with the Sourahs, who generally make their attacks under the cover of darkness, a mode of warfare which the Khond seldom puts into practice.

The Sourahs do not sacrifice human beings, nor is female infanticide known among them, but some of them participate in the Meriah, by procuring flesh from places where the sacrifice occurs, and burying it in their fields. They did not seem to attach much importance to the rite, and at once promised to have nothing more to say to it even as spectators.

From Godairy, where I left some sick

men, I proceeded on the 14th of January
in a north-easterly direction, over an unexplored country, and by difficult paths to
Lumbargam, of " Mal Moota," of Godairy.
Lumbargam is one of a cluster of six villages, each occupying a distinct basin or
dell, surrounded by rugged wooded mountains, communicating with each other by
paths difficult for any but a mountaineer to
travel.　These villages 'are generally at feud
with each other, but on the occasion of my
visit, they were closely united to repel the
retribution which they supposed I had come
to exact for the murders in which all were
more or less concerned, of the three messen-
gers of the " Nigoban " manager of Godairy, who under cover of being the
bearers of a proclamation respecting the
Meriah, had extorted buffaloes, goats, and
brass vessels from the Khonds.

It is not easy adequately to convey a just notion of the patience, perseverance, and forbearance required in dealing with these wild people, suspicious to a degree, easily moved to violence, and acting apparently more from animal instinct than the reasoning of human beings. For eleven days I was encamped in rice fields, which, during that time, were twice flooded with rain. I had also to cut a way, not without considerable difficulty, through the jungle, over two ghats, leading to three of the principal villages, in order to communicate with, and undeceive the people. Either they did not comprehend me, or there was some underhand influence at work which I could not detect. These Khonds were of the wildest I had yet met with; their country has no superfluity of produce for sale or barter, and they seldom leave their own

K

bounds except to fight with some neighbouring tribe, which they are prone to do
on very slight provocation. After repeated
threats and demonstrations, emboldened
by the smallness of the force at my disposal, about three hundred of them attacked
my camp, shouting and yelling more like
demons than men. The attacking party
were supported by as many more, uttering
cries of encouragement from the rocks and
jungle which surrounded the camp, but a
steady and resolute advance soon drove
them off. A few shots completed the rout,
and we pursued them rapidly over the
mountains till they were lost in the jungle
dells on the other side.

The next day delegates arrived from the
several villages of the confederation, and
the day following all came in, made their
submission, delivered up thirty-three Me-

riahs, and entered into the usual agreement to forsake the sacrifice of human beings for ever. Confidence was established, and my camp crowded with our late foes, gazing with astonishment at all they saw. The Chief of Lumbargam, Brino Maji, who had been the first to submit, had the " Sari " or turban conferred him, a token of recognition on the part of Government and of fealty on his.

The whole neighbouring population were intensely watching the result of the struggle at Lumbargam, the successful termination of which exercised a most favourable influence on the proceedings which followed in the large " Moota " of Sirdapore, where the Khonds declared that they might as well fight against the sun !

From Lumbargam I proceeded in a southerly direction, in three marches, by the most difficult paths I ever travelled, to Sirdapore, where all the Khonds were ready to wait upon me, with the exception of those of Dagodi, who on the third day after my arrival, came in with the Meriahs, and from them I learnt that they had bribed one of the inferior Ooryah officers of the district, who had considerable influence with them, to keep me from their village, and so enable them to retain their Meriahs. I caused the amount of the bribe to be repaid in my presence, and sent the offender to his master the Rajah of Jeypore.

I found Sirdapore distracted by internal feuds, many lives had been lost, villages burned, and a considerable portion of the land left uncultivated for several seasons to the great distress of the people. These feuds I had the happiness of healing. I

also settled many desperate dissensions of
old standing in other parts of the Khond
country, and thus restored to the villages
and fields several hundred families, who
had been driven by their more powerful
opponents to take shelter in the jungles,
where they were exposed to great hardships,
living in temporary huts, raised in unas-
sailable positions, and subsisting on such
jungle fruits and roots as they could find.
Where the disputants are more equally
matched, the feud is kept alive by their
plundering each other of cattle, and by
acts of hostility; for although all parties
may be most desirous of a settlement, it is
not easy to bring them together. Indeed,
it has occurred repeatedly that the very men
who have come secretly to me begging that
I would compose their quarrel, have been
the loudest to disclaim in public all desire

for an arrangement, preferring, as they said, to fight it out.

When, however, the parties agreed to submit their feuds to my arbitration, I assembled the chiefs of as many neutral tribes and Ooryah Paturs as were within reach, and forming a sort of court under some convenient tree, I heard from each side the origin and details of the quarrel, the number of cattle taken, and the number of lives lost by each. The latter I generally found very evenly balanced, for they are very unwilling to admit having lost more men than their adversary, and account only for those openly slain. Those who have been waylaid and secretly murdered are passed over as having been devoured by a tiger or snake. There is of course much loud and angry disputations, but eventually the record of their respective losses in cattle or articles, reckoned by knots on a cord made from the bark of a tree having been handed to me, I called upon the Khond and Ooryah chiefs to give their opinion as to what the award should be; and this being duly pronounced and settled, the opponents are then brought together, swear eternal friendship, hug and embrace each other, and receiving from me a small money present, they return to their homes rejoicing that they can now go to their occupations without fear of being waylaid.

The people of Sirdapore, with the exception of two or three villages bordering on Chinna Kimedy are on a par in point of civilization with the Khonds of Bissum Cuttack and the lower parts of Godairy. They do not rear Meriahs as in many other places, but procure Meriah flesh from Ryabiji and Chunderpore.

When a sacrifice is considered necessary, they unite and purchase a victim for the occasion; but at once, without any hesitation, they agreed to abandon the rite and all participation in it for ever. They came freely into my camp, and I have no reason to doubt the sincerity of their promise.

On the 6th of February I returned to Godiary to procure provisions and to forward the work of the bungalow. From thence I marched in four days by Seirgooda, Bijipore, Kiloondi to Chunderpore, one of the strongholds of the Meriah, second only to Ryabiji. The Khonds came to me much more readily than on my first visit a few weeks before, and delivered up their Meriahs. Several of the Khond chiefs on being asked to sign the pledge, which was always carefully explained to them, to abandon the sacrifice answered,

" Many countries have forsaken the Meriah sacrifice at the orders of the Great Government, why should not we do so also ?"

The people of Bundari, one of the principal Khond villages of this " Moota," refused to come to me, or send me their Meriahs. They fled with every thing they could remove to their concealed fastnesses in the mountains, which I failed to discover. In riding in the direction of Bundari I there found the cause of flight. A post spotted with blood, to which a victim had been fastened by the hair, the head still suspended from the post to which the sacrificial knife was attached. This piteous sight agitated the whole camp, and all felt they could not leave Bundari till the five victims still in the possession of these barbarians were rescued.

The sacrifice which had taken place, called " Junna," is performed as follows, and is always succeeded by the sacrifice of three other human victims, two to the sun to the east and west, and one in the centre, with the usual barbarities. A stout wooden post is firmly fixed in the ground, at the foot of it a narrow grave is dug, and to the top of the post the victim is firmly fastened by the long hair of his head. Four assistants hold his outstretched arms and legs, the body being suspended horizontally over the grave with the face towards the earth. The officiating " zani," priest, standing on the right side, repeats the following invocation, at intervals hacking with his sacrificing knife the back part of the shrieking victim's neck:

" O, mighty Manicksoro, this is your

festal day." (To the Khonds the offering
is 'Meriah,' to the Rajahs ' Junna.') "On
account of this sacrifice you have given to
rajahs countries, guns, and swords. The
sacrifice we now offer you must eat, and
we pray that our battle-axes may be turned
into swords, our bows and arrows into gun-
powder and balls, and if we have any quarrels with other tribes, give us the victory,
and preserve us from the tyranny of rajahs
and their officers."

Then addressing the victim, "That we
may enjoy prosperity, we offer you a sacrifice to our God Manicksoro, who will immediately eat you, so be not grieved at our
slaying you. Your parents were aware
when we purchased you from them for sixty
'gunties,' (articles) that we did so with
intent to sacrifice you; there is therefore
no sin on our heads but on your parents.

After you are dead we shall perform your obsequies."

The victim is then decapitated, the body thrown into the grave, and the head left suspended from the post till devoured by wild beasts. The knife remains fastened to the post till the three sacrifices already mentioned have been performed, when it is removed with much ceremony. The knife and post used in the sacrifice I have alluded to, are now in my possession.

I used every exertion to communicate with the people. I even offered them pardon for the grievous offence they had committed, but it was of no avail. Provisions became scarce, sickness prevailed to an alarming extent, and as the only means of saving the lives of the three victims whose sacrifice would have assuredly followed that which had been already perpetrated,

I most reluctantly ordered the village of
Bundari to be burnt, and also eight posts,
the relics of former sacrifices, to be destroyed. The successful evasion of this
people would, if unpunished, have set a
most injurious example to the whole sacrificing population.

Leaving Bundari on the 24th of February, I passed through the secondary
range of hills of Chinna Kimedy, inhabited
by sacrificing tribes, and was gratified to
find that they continued true to their
pledge of forsaking the Meriah rite.

The lateness of the season, and the difficulty of procuring a sufficiency of water
for my camp in the infanticidal " Maliahs,"
prevented my visiting those tribes, but on
my arrival in Soorada, below the ghats,
many of the chiefs and a great number of
the Meriah females who had been married

to Khonds of these tracts, visited me with their children, to receive the usual presents of clothes, &c., and from them I learned with satisfaction that female children were now generally preserved, and in cases where they were destroyed, it was done with great secresy, and not openly as in former times. The officer I had employed in superintending them, confirmed this report.

The number of real Meriahs rescued this season was one hundred and fifty-eight, the number of "Possiahs," registered and restored to their owners, sixteen.

It is deserving of remark that four Khonds, who had formed attachments to Meriah women, fled with them to my camp for protection in Jeypore, preferring to forsake their country and people, rather than that their wives (as they may be called) and children should run the risk of being sacrificed. Two Khond women also fled from Bundari with Meriah youths, from motives of humanity as they stated to me, but I think they were influenced by a more tender feeling. Several other similar instances occurred in my various journeys, but not to the extent which might have been expected, owing to a belief generally entertained by the Meriahs that having once partaken of "Meriah food," rice, turmeric, &c., prepared with certain ceremonies, they have no longer any inclination to escape, as the following incident will illustrate.

In 1839, three young women of the Panoo caste of the plains were hired by a seller of salt-fish and salt, to carry his merchandise into the Khond "Maliahs," where having sold his goods, the villain sold the women also. On the complaint of their relations, they were sought after, recovered and sent to me by Sam Bissoi, chief of Hodzaghur.   On my questioning them, they said they had twice attempted to escape, but were brought back where the Khonds compelled them to eat of the Meriah food, after which they became reconciled to their fate, and lost all inclination to escape.

The districts of Rýabiji and Chunderpore have been the strongholds of the Meriah sacrifice in Jeypore.   Out of the one hundred and fifty-eight Meriahs of the season, one hundred and four were from these two districts.   They have now been traversed throughout.   We know all the principal villages, and their chiefs, and they know something of us, and of our object in coming to them.   The first operations among a wild and strange people, always the most difficult and most hazardous, having been successful, those of succeeding seasons, if the same principles are adhered to, are mere gleanings, but the perils of the climate must always remain the same.

The Meriah females were more eagerly sought after in marriage by the Khonds of Sooradah and Chinna Kimedy than formerly, and several have been married to Meriah youths, settled as "Ryuts," in Goomsur and elsewhere.

The Meriah families, formerly settled as "Ryuts" in Goomsur, are doing well. About a third of the number—those originally established—have this year, for the first time, paid the rent of their land. From a third, the full amount was collected, but remitted, to support them till next harvest, and for seed. And a third, more recently settled, are maintained at the expense

of the State. By the next harvest, I anticipate that nearly all will be in a condition
to support themselves; but they are generally idle, restraint of any kind is distasteful
to them, and they miss their favourite
toddy, and the many esculent roots which
abound in the mountain forests.

Sickness was, as usual, this season our
deadliest foe. My escort of native troops
was soon disabled, and *hors de combat.* I
had no alternative but to send them to the
plains. I need not say how much my
movements were crippled, nor could I have
accomplished what I did but for the invaluable aid of my own faithful Irregulars,
who were well acclimated, and fit for anything.

Of the few European officers with the
regular troops, one died of fever, and the
other three were sent off to various cli-

mates, in search of the health they had lost in the Hills.

I remained, during the rainy season, when residence in the Hills is impossible, at Berampore and Gopaulpore on the sea-coast; and with my establishment, endeavoured so to recruit our healths, as to enable us again to take the field when the season permitted.

CHAPTER VIII.

THE month of November, 1852, found me once more in the Soorada infanticidal tracts, where I passed some time, and personally examined into the condition of the people. I went to five villages, and ascertained the number of children under five years of age in each family, and having thus obtained accurate information to this extent, I deputed a practised and intelligent man of my establishment to go leisurely from village to village, counting the houses and families in each, and the number of female children, under five years of age, in each family.

Wherever I halted, mothers with their children assembled round my tent, and I showed special favour, and made presents —handsome, in their eyes—to those who had female children. To each I gave four or five yards of stout cotton cloth, and to the children, strings of coloured glass beads. Combs and small looking-glasses were also distributed to laughing mothers and screaming children, who were freely admitted to my tent, which, with its contents, they examined with wonder, frequently exclaiming to each other, "It is the house of a god."

Small-pox commits great havoc throughout these hills. I endeavoured to introduce vaccination, but only with partial success; though such was the confidence entertained of our skill and desire to benefit them, that sick persons, young and old, were brought to the paths by which I was expected to pass, in hopes of receiving something to cure them.

From the infanticidal tribes, I passed into the country of the sacrificing tribes of Chinna Kimedy, where I succeeded in capturing the actual perpetrators of, and several of the principal participators in a sacrifice which was performed last season. I was also fortunate in preventing a sacrifice at the village of Bondigam, for which a victim and all necessary accessories had been hastily provided; but timely information enabled me to rescue the victim, a girl of about six years old, two hours only before the time appointed for her immolation. Some days after, I secured the leaders in the proposed outrage.

The interrupted sacrifice was not premeditated, but arose from a sudden temptation, which these wild people could not resist. They had, some years before, paid a sum of money to a Panoo of Guddapore, to provide them with a Meriah. In the meantime came the orders prohibiting human sacrifice, and the Panoo evaded the fulfilment of his agreement. This year the Khonds were pressing, and insisted on their money being returned; the Panoo, not having the money, or, possibly, calculating that the Khonds would not dare to sacrifice, gave them his own daughter, Ootoma. But he was mistaken; the temptation was too great, the earth deity seemed to have provided the blood which had been interdicted her, and the Khonds of Bondigam at once determined on the sacrifice, which was so happily prevented.

My new assistant, Lieutenant MacNeill, was successful in the western part of Chinna Kimedy, where he seized three chiefs, the joint pepetrators of a sacrifice at Solavesca of Baracooma, part of the flesh of which was brought to the Khond chiefs of Possunga, who received it ; but they afterwards came to me voluntarily in a body ready, as they said, to endure any punishment I chose to inflict, for they had broken their pledge, and had been tempted to receive the forbidden flesh.

The ready submission of these wild men,

when they could have easily evaded me, and their simple confession of wrong, clearly indicated the proper course to be pursued towards them. After impressing on their mind that the participators in Meriah flesh were equally guilty with the actual sacrificers, I dismissed them to their villages, detaining only the Khond who had brought the forbidden flesh to Possunga.

In every district there is a party sincerely disposed to abandon the sacrifice of human beings. There are also some untameable spirits, whom nothing but severity can restrain from their ancient murderous rite. Such persons say,

" What can he do to us ? he won't burn our villages, nor shoot us. When we threaten him he only tries to catch us, and it is our own fault if he does that."

I afterwards procured the submission of

the only "Mootas" in Chinna Kimedy that were in opposition, Toopunga and Parighur. From Parighur, four Meriahs and fourteen "Possiahs" were delivered to me.

These last, to the very great contentment of the people, being the wives, originally purchased as Meriahs, and children of three of the principal chiefs of the "Moota," were at once restored; and I learnt that it was from fear that these cherished ones should be removed, that they were deterred from earlier making their submission, and pledging themselves as they now did with much apparent sincerity to abandon the sacrifice of human beings for ever.

A very different spirit actuated the people of Toopunga, inhabiting a rugged country, and very difficult of access. This people are a wild, unruly set; they had been long at variance with the Ooryah chief of Shoobernagery, and though summoned by us for three successive seasons, they refused to come or give up their Meriahs. They were determined to fight, and having a high character for courage among the neighbouring tribes, it was absolutely necessary for the success of my operations, endangered by this bold defiance, to bring the question to an issue.

After a toilsome night march, I arrived early in the morning with a small party of my Irregulars at the principal cluster of villages of Toopunga. I endeavoured to parley with the people, but the only reply I received was threats of destruction, and of making a Meriah of me if I did not instantly quit their territory; and, accordingly when the warriors of the tribe assembled—

summoned together by the sounding of horns—they came pouring down upon me through the jungle in several parties, evidently bent on trying the question with their battle-axes. In self defence, and much against my will, I was compelled to fire. The courage of the men of Toopunga failed, and they fled leaving their villages, (from which all property had been removed some days before,) to the mercy of the excited followers of the Ooryah chief of Shoobernagery who accompanied me, and who, with the matches of their matchlock guns, set fire to three small villages.

Soon after the Khonds of Toopunga hastened to Buchadar Patur, the Ooryah chief of the district, with their Meriahs, and entreated him to intercede with me for pardon. They then made unconditional submission.

Although I regretted the attack made
upon me by the people, the result had a
marked and salutary effect not only on
Toopunga, but on the whole of the sacrificing tribes of Chinna Kimedy. Many of
the Khond chiefs expressed the greatest
satisfaction at the punishment with which
the audacious tribe of Toopunga had been
visited, and all the Ooryah chiefs were
unanimous in declaring that nothing had
been wanting for the final suppression of
the Meriah sacrifice but an unmistakeable
manifestation of the determination of Government to put an end to it. They could
now, they said, speak with authority to
their Khonds, and point to Toopunga as a
warning to those who opposed the orders
of Government for the suppression of the
Meriah.

From Chinna Kimedy, I proceeded to

Bundari of Jeypore. I found the people anxiously looking for my arrival, uncertain as to their reception, in consequence of the sacrifice perpetrated by them last year —as already related—and the destruction of their village, a measure to which I had been forced, as the only means of averting the fate of three victims in their possession, and doomed for sacrifice. They soon, however, gained confidence, and came to me with their Meriahs, throwing themselves on the mercy of the Government. Of the three victims intended for sacrifice, one had made his escape to my camp, another had died, and the third, a young woman who had undergone the usual preliminary ceremonies, and being the property of the community, they requested might be removed, lest her presence should prove a temptation, as they were determined to abandon the sacrifice of human beings for ever. Two others, young girls of twelve and fourteen were delivered to me, with the earnest desire that they might be given in marriage to two young Khonds of the village. To this I agreed, on the usual securities being taken, and they were betrothed in my presence.

The chiefs then signed the pledge to forsake the Meriah rite, received back the grain which I had caused to be removed, when their village was destroyed, and a handsome present of money to assist in rebuilding it. The whole assembly admitted the justice of the punishment which had been inflicted on the people of Bundari, and wondered at the liberality and mercy of the Great Government towards the penitent offenders.

Before leaving Bundari I was requested

by the chiefs to erect a post on the site of the new village which they were about to build, as a mark that it was sanctioned by authority. I accordingly rode to the site of the old village, but the chiefs came in haste, exclaiming, "Not there; that ground has been accustomed for many years to human blood, and will continue to demand more—we will build on new ground." I followed where they led, and on the spot pointed out, erected a substantial post amidst the shouts and rejoicings of men, women and children.

From Bundari I moved to Ryabiji, where I remained several days, receiving the Khonds of the district who came in crowds to visit me. The principal village of Rya-biji had been deserted for several years, and its inhabitants living in small hamlets scattered around, were contemplating the

building of a new Ryabiji, the old town
having been abandoned, as the people told
me, on account of its having been taken
possession of by demons, who had brought
death and disease to their families and
flocks. I was solicited to mark the spot to
be fixed on as the centre of the new village,
which I did, and ordered a display of roc-
kets and fireworks in the evening, to the
great delight of the people who had never
seen anything of the kind before.

From the Ooryah Patur of this district,
I rescued three Junna youths who were intended for sacrifice on the building of this
village. In presence of all the Khonds of
the district, the Junnas were delivered to
me by the Patur, who in the most energetic manner abjured the rite, and called
upon them to witness the abjuration, and
to admire the virtue of this gentleman

M

(meaning myself) who made no distinction in administering justice between Ooryah and Khond,

From Ryabiji I marched to Godairy, and thus having passed through the strong-holds of the Meriah in Jeypore, I was gratified to find that out of two hundred and twenty Khond villages, only one chief, Larunga, Maji of Dadojoringi, refused to produce his Meriahs; and he alone of all the Khonds of Jeypore performed the Meriah sacrifice last year after I had left the country.

This sacrifice had been attended by a comparatively small number of people, and these were disgusted with an extra piece of barbarity, distasteful even to them. After the victims, a man and a woman, had been sacrificed, and whilst their remains were being thrown into the hole prepared for them, a child of the woman, about three years old, crept near this Maji, when the monster seized him by the legs, and whirling him round his head dashed him into the grave, where he was buried with the mangled remains of his mother.

It afforded me much satisfaction to see the confidence with which these wild men of Jeypore now visited my camp on this my second appearance among them, showing a remarkable contrast to their shyness of last season; even my old opponents of Lumbargam, Serdapore, and Bapella, came a distance of twenty-four miles to see me.

To some of the most intelligent of the Khond chiefs I offered to restore their Meriahs for adoption, but they refused to receive them back, alleging that they would be a temptation to the people. A more convincing proof of the progress made in

M 2

weaning these people from their ancient rite could not be desired.

At this place, my assistant joined me from the jungly "Mootas" of Lunkagher, Goomagur, and Goonjideso of Chinna Kimedy, where he was going on very successfully, when sickness compelled him to leave for a more open part of the country, bringing with him forty Meriah victims.

The inhabitants of the "Mootas" above named, are a wild race known as Kootia Khonds, speaking a dialect of the Khond language differing considerably from that spoken by the surrounding tribes. They have very little rice cultivation, use no ploughs, and subsist chiefly on the different kinds of pulse and other dry grains grown in patches on the slopes of the hills.

From Godairy I sent the greater part of my escort, who were suffering from fever, with my assistant back to the plains through the lower part of the Chinna Kimedy "Maliahs," and proceeded myself on the 12th of January, 1853, to Bissum Cuttack of Jeypore, where I found the Khonds under their zealous and energetic ruler, Nairraindur Deo, in perfect tranquillity and true to their pledge.

From Bissum Cuttack I pursued my course to Calahundi of Nagpore, with the intention of visiting Tooamool, a hill principality, tributary to Calahundi, the chief of which was under restraint at Nagpore, charged among other offences, with encouraging, or conniving at the performance of the Meriah sacrifice among his Khonds, but I found Tooamool in such a state of anarchy, and the people so ex-

asperated against the Rajah of Calahundi,
that it would have been worse than useless
to have entered the country for Meriah
suppression purposes. In the absence of
their own chief, I should have been looked
upon as a partizan of the Rajah of Calahundi, and in that supposed character there
was much risk of my being brought into
collision with the Khonds and other inhabitants who were 'prepared to resist, as
they had already done, even the authority
of His Highness the Rajah of Nagpore.

From Calahundi I passed through a considerable portion of the Khond country of
the Patna Zumindari, and satisfied myself
that the Meriah sacrifice had not within the
memory of man existed to a greater extent
than the sacrifice of one or two victims
throughout the whole country once in five
or six years. Patna is not a mountainous

country, it has vast plains, now but partially
cultivated, yet bearing the marks of former
extensive cultivation in numerous remains
of tanks and rice embankments.

At some distance from a village called
Soorada, may be seen a remarkable collec-
tion of pagodas, which I visited, and
counted one hundred and twenty of various
dimensions. They were built of cut stone,
without cement, and most of them are in a
state of dilapidation. On the largest tem-
ple is some writing in the "Devi Nagari"
character, but now illegible. In the centre
of this group of pagodas was a circle two
hundred and ten feet in circumference, surrounded by a wall of cut stone, twelve feet
high, with sixty-five niches on the inner
side, containing sixty figures of goddesses
in a variety of attitudes, and in the centre
of the circle, placed on a raised platform,

sat a remarkable figure, tolerably carved, as were also the others, in stone. Few of these deities were recognised by my people, though among them were two Brahmins. The tradition here is, that these temples were built by magicians, and the guide, who pointed out the way, would not go within two miles of them. Even my own people were rather uneasy. The conclusion that I came to was, that this part of the country must have been occupied by a race of Hindoos, of whom there is now no trace. It is now thinly inhabited by a comparatively civilized people, who call themselves Khonds, though they do not speak their dialect. Their language and dress are Ooryah, and they are very industrious.

From Patna I passed into the small hill, Zumendari of Muddenpore, tributary to Calahundi, and found it distracted by internal dissensions, owing to a departure from the regular line of succession to the chieftainship, in the person of the youngest brother of the recently deceased chief, instead of the elder brother, who is, unhappily, a leper. Though thus disagreeing among themselves, they professed obedience to the British Government, and delivered up the last of their Meriahs.

The Rajah of Calahundi, or Kirond, Futty Narrain Deo, a well educated and superior man, was with me for some days, and promised to use his best endeavours to effect a compromise between the brothers, by fixing the succession on the son of the leper, at the death of the present chief.

From Muddenpore of Calahundi, I proceeded to Mahasingi of Chinna Kimedy, halting at several places by the way, to receive the visits of the Khonds, talk to

them, settle their disputes, and make en-
quiries respecting the Meriah.

At Mahasingi, I met by appointment
twenty-two Ooryah and Khond chiefs of
districts and "Mootas" of Chinna Kimedy,
and after considerable discussion, succeeded
in settling several blood feuds of long
standing, some of them respecting boundaries, which I marked out. Before leaving, I strongly impressed upon the chiefs,
and succeeded in convincing them, that
dissensions among themselves materially
weakened their authority over their people.
At parting, I presented them with silver
anklets and bracelets, silk, cloth, and cotton
shawls, according to their rank.

These men had rendered most essential
services, for several years, in their respective districts. To the cordial co-operation
of the Ooryah, and the ready acquiescence

of the Khond chiefs, we owe much of the
success which has attended our operations.
They have been put to great, but unavoidable, inconvenience by their attendance on
my movements, and have exposed themselves to a considerable amount of obloquy
for their ready assent to the views of
Government. They had hitherto received
no reward or remuneration beyond the
usual subsistence money for themselves and
followers, when employed on the public
service. These silver anklets and bracelets
are greatly prized by the Hill chiefs as
marks of distinction, and it is very desirable
that they should be encouraged to continue
the valuable aid they are so capable of
rendering.

From Mahasingi of Chinna Kimedy I proceeded into the Boad " Maliahs." Throughout, the Khonds came crowding to see their

"father," and I recognised many familiar faces among the men who hurried on to clear the paths of jungle and other obstacles, shouting and laughing as they went.

During my stay in Boad, I learnt with great satisfaction that the Meriah sacrifice was not even spoken of among the Khonds, that the whole land had repudiated the cruel rite, and that there had not been a human victim slain since 1847. I also took the opportunity of examining a considerable portion of the road which had just been finished between Goomsur and Sohunpore on the Mahanuddi. It is difficult fully to appreciate the value of this road, both as a line of traffic into Nagpore as well as to the inhabitants of Chinna Kimedy and Boad. Already was the road well frequented by " Brinjaries," carrying cotton and wheat to the coast. About twenty thousand bullocks have passed this season, and will return again laden with salt. The Khond inhabitants instead of waiting in their villages for the arrival of the travelling merchants, who annually visit them to purchase horns, oil seeds, turmeric, and other produce, now carry these articles to the weekly markets on the plains, obtain better prices, and purchase what they may require at more reasonable rates. I met several large parties of Khonds and Ooryahs going to the fair, and among them a good many women, who, until the opening of the road, had never ventured on the journey.

The rescued Meriah victims, settled as cultivators, are now, I am happy to say, acquiring regular habits of industry. About thirty of them were employed throughout the season in the construction of the Sohunpore road.

The number of Meriahs rescued this season is one hundred and fifty, and one hundred "Possiahs," or serfs, were registered and restored to their owners.

The operations of this season were brought to a close in March, 1853, when, wearied with our labours and worn with incessant fever, which spares no one in those hills, myself and the Agency establishment returned to the low country.

CHAPTER IX.

ALL THE TRIBES OF UPPER AND LOWER CHINNA KIMEDY
VISITED—THEIR PROSPERITY AND INCREASING FAMI-
LIARITY — READ PROCLAMATION — REPLY OF KHOND
CHIEFS—DELIVERY OF RUNAWAY MERIAHS—CAPTURE
OF A NOTORIOUS KIDNAPPER—RECEPTION AT JRYPORE
—NO SACRIFICE THERE SINCE 1852—RYAGHUR AND
LINKAPORE—SOME ACCOUNT OF THEM—TOOMOOL—SICK-
NESS—ACCOUNT OF PEOPLE AND COUNTRY—BUNDUSIR
—RAJAH PUTTY NARAIN DEO OF KALAHUND—CONCLUDING
REMARKS.

THOUGH still suffering from the effects
of fever it was imperative that no season
should pass without our presence amongst
the various Hill tribes. Accordingly, in
November, 1853, I prepared for what

proved to be my last campaign in the Khond Tracts.

On my way to Chinna Kimedy I paid a short visit to the Infanticidal tribes, and was satisfied that to some extent they now rear their infant female children. The complete suppression of this practice must be the work of time and careful super-vision.

The lower and 'upper ranges of the Chinna Kimedy mountains were visited by myself and my assistant. We met every tribe, not one evaded us, nor was one village deserted, as in former years.

The Khonds assembled in crowds in our respective camps, and with a freedom never before evinced by them ; selling or exchanging with our people the produce of their fields, for money, salt, bread, or pieces of cloth. After they had completed their barter, the chiefs of "Mootas" and villages with their people assembled round our tents, and listened attentively to the reading of a proclamation in the Khond dialect, reiterating the prohibition of the sacrifice of human beings, and permitting them to substitute animals instead. Copies of this proclamation were left in every "Moota." Each chief was invited freely to express his sentiments on this proclamation, which many did without hesitation, saying,

"When you first came among us we were like beasts in the jungle, doing as our fathers had done; but we now clearly comprehend that your only object in coming is to stop human sacrifice. Not a fowl or anything else has been taken from us, not even a fence injured by the people of your camp. Our fields produce crops as

N

good as formerly, and sickness is not more prevalent. Our Meriahs have been all removed, and now we are of one mind, determined never more to have anything to do with human sacrifice. Moreover, it is no use resisting the orders of the Great Government."

In two or three places it was asked, "What are we to say to the deity?" They were told they might say whatever they pleased. Then one of the chiefs repeated the following formula: "Do not be angry with us, O, goddess, for giving you the blood of beasts instead of human blood, but vent your wrath on this gentleman, who is well able to bear it. We are guiltless."

Seventeen Meriahs only have been found this season in the whole of Chinna Kimedy, and these were delivered up voluntarily by their owners. Nine Meriahs who had deserted from villages on the plains wherein they had been located, were either given up, or surrendered themselves because their former owners would not receive them. One of these young men on being remonstrated with, on the risk he had run of suffering a cruel and painful death, replied, "It is better to be sacrificed as a Meriah among my own people and give them pleasure, than to live on the plains. Am I not a Meriah?"

Thirty-seven Possia women, who had been purchased when very young, were with their children (sixty-three in number) registered and restored to their husbands.

I succeeded in effecting the capture of Buddo Mundo, a notorious kidnapper of children, who last year had sold his own daughter Ootoma as already related. She is now with other rescued Meriahs under the care of the missionaries at Berhampore, and is a child of rare intelligence, and of the most affectionate disposition.

In the Khond tracts of Jeypore my reception was most gratifying. I visited my old opponents of Lumbargam, Bapola and Bundare, and found them contented and happy; they, with all the Khonds of Jeypore, declaring their fidelity to the pledge they had taken.

Two Meriah women who had been given in marriage to Khonds of the Soorada Infanticidal tribes, and who had fled from their husbands, were given up, and a Meriah youth who had escaped from me last season was brought back by his owner, Indromooni Maji of Ryabiji, a fine intelligent Khond. This chief reproached me for having allowed him to escape, for, said he, " he has undergone the ceremonies preparatory to sacrifice, and therefore is a temptation to us; take him away with you." This, among similar instances, shews that it is not a fact as has been stated, that " a Meriah victim once in the possession of, or produced before a Government officer is a victim no longer, his atoning efficacy destroyed, his sacred character profaned, there is no fear after this pollution of his being sent to the stake;" and I have already mentioned three instances where Meriahs were sacrificed after having been in the possession of Government officers.

There has been no sacrifice, nor attempt to sacrifice in Jeypore since March, 1852.

From Jeypore I passed in a north-westerly direction through the Zumendaries of Ryaghur and Linkapore, a fine, open, level country, and well cultivated. The population consists of Khonds and Tellogoos. The

Khonds are an industrious and civilised race, and pay rent for their land like their Tellogoo neighbours. They acknowledged having occasionally procured the flesh of a victim from Jeypore, but for many years no sacrifice had taken place among themselves. Through these Zumindaries upwards of twenty thousand "Brinjary" bullocks pass from the interior to the coast with oil seeds, wheat and cotton, and return laden with salt.

From Linkapore I sent my assistant through the hilly country of Bundasir of Calahundi, inhabited by sacrificing tribes of Khonds, while I turned nearly west towards Tooamool. Sickness had for some days been on the increase in my camp, and at the second march into the mountain ranges of Tooamool, increased greatly. The doctor in medical charge of the camp,

and the officer commanding my escort of
sepoys, being added to the list with severe
fever. I was therefore compelled—while
it was yet possible to procure carriage for
the sick—to send them all back to the low
country, where I am glad to say they
arrived in safety.

Tooamool which we reached by a succession of difficult ghats, is on the table-land
of a high range of mountains, in length
about thirty-two miles east and west, and
in breadth about fourteen. The climate is
very trying; the thermometer in my tent
at six o'clock in the morning ranged from
35° to 38°, and at noon from 81° to 83°;
we had often hoar frost and thin ice, which
was there seen for the first time by my native followers.

The inhabitants subsist on different kinds
of maize, grown on the slopes of their hills,

which are almost cleared of jungle, and cultivated to the top. Their rice cultivation is very scanty. The crops this season had failed in these high regions, as well as in the plains, so I had great difficulty in supplying even my reduced camp, and we were frequently on half rations.

I found the Khonds tractable and well disposed, though at first somewhat alarmed, but they soon gained confidence, and men, women, and children came into my camp freely. They had never seen a European before, and my tent and its contents, elephants and horses, were great attractions.

I ascertained beyond a doubt that the Khonds of Tooamool did not rear Meriahs, but when they had determined on a sacrifice, they applied to the Tat Rajah, who sold to them some unfortunate person accused of sorcery, from sums varying from twenty to fifty rupees.

After the usual meetings and consultations, and frequent palavers amongst the chiefs, they in the presence of their people signed the pledge to forsake the Meriah right for ever. They declared that no sacrifice had taken place since the removal of their Tat Rajah, three years ago, to Nagpore, where he lately died a prisoner.

"They had heard," they said, " that the 'Company'"—they knew the mysterious name—" had sent a great officer to the Khonds of Jeypore, and Chinna Kimedy, to abolish the Meriah sacrifice, and they had felt disappointed that no officer had been sent to them. They were now, however, pleased to find that they were held in equal estimation with their brethren of other countries."

At Koorlapaut, a tributary of Calahundi, on the same mountain range as Tooamool, the Khonds came to me with perfect confidence. They made a statement with respect to the Meriah, similar to that given by the Khonds of Tooamool.

My assistant, who traversed the Khond mountains of Bundasir of Calahundi, found the Khonds most submissive and tractable. Formerly when they required a sacrifice, they purchased a victim from some distant country, but the Rajah of Calahundi, Futty Narrain Deo having forbidden the Meriah, and twice punished them very severely, once for sacrificing, and a second time for attempting to sacrifice, they were resolved to give it up, and now that the Great Government had sent an officer to them, they were confirmed in that resolution. In plain fact, they knew from the experience of their neighbours, that no opposition was likely to be effective.

To this Rajah, Futty Narrain Deo, great credit is due, for his earnest and effectual efforts for the suppression of human sacrifices in the Hill Zumindaries, under his authority; and all that was required for the perfecting of his work, was the personal communication which I have now had with his Khonds; impressing them with the wholesome conviction that not only are they responsible to their Rajah, but also to the Government, whose officers have penetrated into all their fastnesses.

In Calahundi I met several large droves of " Brinjary" bullocks proceeding to the coast for salt; their owners complained bitterly of the heavy transit dues levied from them by the different petty Zumindars, or landed proprietors, through whose territory they passed, amounting in the aggregate to nearly half the price paid by them at the sea-coast for their salt. The Zumindars keep the paths by which the cattle travel tolerably clear, and protect the Brinjaries from molestation, though they are well able to take care of themselves.

Could the population which has been driven away by famine and disease be replaced, the vast pláins of Calahundi and lower Patna, now lying waste, studded with ancient temples and ruined tanks, might become as rich and productive in cotton and other crops as the most fertile parts of Nagpore.

The narrative of the operations which brought to a close this season's labour, speaks for itself. The Khonds every where were making sure and certain progress in their complete emancipation from the cruel rite of human sacrifices which for ages had prevailed amongst them.

It was destined that my humble but earnest labour amongst these Mountains tribes of Khondistan should this season terminate for ever; but I can never cease to feel the warmest and most heartfelt interest in their welfare. My work in these hills was always to me a labour of love, and I linger with affectionate remembrance on the many years I lived among them, and pitched my tent in their mountain villages.

I will only ask the reader's patience for one more chapter, and then "my tale is told."

CHAPTER X.

IT will not, I hope, be supposed from
the imperfect narrative which I have traced
that the Hill tribes upon any occasion, and
more especially in the early days of our
intercourse with them, readily yielded to
our wishes, and abandoned their ancient
rite. On the contrary, long days and
nights of almost interminable discussion
invariably preceded any surrender on their
parts ; but I have not deemed it needful to

exhaust the reader's patience with a constant repetition of these very necessary, but most wearying, councils and debates.

The first step of progress was to gain the favourable opinion of the low country rulers, or rajahs. It is impossible accurately to define the exact position of these little magnates to their Hill subjects. It is certain that the former claim an obedience never yielded by the latter, whilst it is equally certain that the Khonds have a strong feeling in favour of the rajah, who, it must be allowed, interferes with them generally as little as possible. He is entitled, equally with their own Hill chiefs, to certain perquisites paid on successions, and sometimes a portion of the fines and forfeits levied on account of offences; but in truth it very much depends upon the temper of the Khonds whether these rajahs ever receive anything. The tribes, however, bestow a certain amount of rice, vegetables, &c., upon any officer deputed by the Rajah to visit them, but they regard this more as a compliment than a matter of right. Indeed they consider that they are completely independant ; they believe themselves the original owners of the land, and pay no rent or taxes to " outsiders," though amongst themselves they sometimes sell or rent their fields—a process fertile in disputes amongst a people without a written language.

Notwithstanding this very vague allegiance, my first step was always to secure the cordial co-operation of the rajahs of the plains, and by visits, presents, and a conciliatory demeanour, I generally achieved my end. These men, like all others, are governed by self-interest, and they soon found that they would be no losers by affording us their influence, limited though it was, to attain our objects amongst their Hill people.

The next and far more important step was to win over the Ooryah chiefs called "Bissois" and "Paturs," according to the district. I have come in contact with sixty-five chiefs in the several divisions of Boad, Chinna Kimedy, Jeypore, and Kalahundy, and I have never removed one from his position.

All were not equally well disposed to forward my views for the suppression of human sacrifice, for they all derived a certain advantage from it, in the shape of offerings from the Khonds on the occasion of a sacrifice; but, notwithstanding this, I did not attempt to subvert their authority, for I knew from experience that anarchy

o

and confusion would have been the result :
I rather, by forbearance and conciliation,
strove to gain their confidence, and to
elevate them both in their own estimation
and in that of their Khonds.

From long hereditary sway their chiefs
exercised considerable influence, and had
the power of moving to much mischief;
or by precept and example smoothing the
way, and satisfying their people of the true
object of our coming among them. The
great point in the first instance was to
bring these wild men into personal communication with me; that difficulty once
overcome, the sure foundation of a successful issue was laid. The Ooryah chiefs
then, were my principal instruments for the
suppression of the Meriah rite, and on
them I chiefly depend for maintaining the
ground we have gained.

As an instance of the hearty co-operation of the Ooryah chiefs, I may mention the conduct of the Tat Rajah, Narraindur Deo, of Bissum Cuttack, who, when informed that his Khonds were preparing to take part in a sacrifice which was performed in March, 1852, in Ryabiji of Jeypore, peremptorily forbade their going, and plainly told them, that if they went, he would waylay them on their return, and shoot every man he could find. Not one went to the place of sacrifice. In other instances, purposed attacks on me were averted by them; and in those I was forced to repel, the Ooryah chiefs, coming in as intercessors for *their discomfited Khonds, acquired new influence—and the submission which followed was complete.

I anticipate highly important results from the diffusion of knowledge, and spread of education among the Khonds, by means of the Meriahs now under instruction in the plains.

The great object I had in view in sending the younger Meriah children, eighty-four girls, and one hundred and sixteen boys, to be educated by the missionaries,* was, that the most intelligent might be brought up as teachers, and eventually settle among their own wild people, where, by precept and example, under the

* Mr. and Mrs. Stubbins, and Mr. and Mrs. Wilkinson, to whom I confided a portion of my young Meriahs, resided at the military station of Berhampore in Ganjam. Mr. and Mrs. Buckley were stationed at Cuttack, in the province of that name, and Mr. Bachelor at Balasore. I have had every reason to be well satisfied with the training bestowed by those worthy people upon the Meriah children.

blessing of God, the pure principles of our holy religion might take root. It was a well-understood part of their education, that they should not be allowed to forget the Khond language, but that it should be cultivated by means of the educational works prepared in that dialect by Captain Frye.

The Government of India have made liberal provision for these young people, both for their present support, and future settlement in life, when their training, either as teachers, artificers, or husbandmen, is completed. Already, some of the elder ones are earning their own livelihood, and some of the young girls have sent me presents of needlework, highly creditable to their aptitude for instruction.

I often endeavoured to obtain accurate information regarding the number of human victims annually sacrificed previous·to our operations. The Khonds, always unwilling to speak on the subject, gave conflicting evidence.

Mr. Ricketts, the commissioner of Cuttack, who, in 1837, rescued sixteen boys and eight girls from the Boad districts, was informed by one Khond that he had witnessed fifty sacrifices, and by another Khond, that he had never seen but three or four.

Captain Macpherson reports in February, 1846, that "about one hundred victims had been immolated in the tracts of Boad, bordering upon Goomsur, in anticipation of the usual season for sacrifice."

The number of Meriah victims rescued during the operations I have sketched, from 1837 to 1854, was one thousand five hundred and six.

	Males.	Females.	Total.
From Goomsur	101	122	223
„ Boad	181	164	345
„ Chinna Kimedy	313	353	666
„ Jeypore	77	116	193
„ Calahundi	43	34	77
„ Patna	2	„	„
	717	789	1,506

And within the same period, eleven hundred and fifty-four " Possias" were registered, and restored to their owners.

The following record will shew how these fifteen hundred and six Merialis have been provided for.

	Males.	Females.	Total.
Restored to relatives and friends, or given for adoption to persons of character in the plains.	194	148	342

	Males.	Females.	Total.
Given in marriage to Khonds and others of suitable condition. . .		267	267
Supporting themselves in public or private service. .	53	22	75
Died.	69	88	157
Deserted. . . .	63	14	77
In Missionary schools at Cuttack, Berhampore and Balasore. . . .	116	84	200
Settled as cultivators in different villages. . .	195	111	306
At the Asylum, Soorada.	27	55	82
	717	789	1506

Among the infanticidal tribes, great progress has been made in weaning them from their cruel practice. The result of the inquiry of 1854, shews a registry of nine hundred and one females under five years of age, in two thousand one hundred and forty-nine families located in villages, where I can state from my own observation that in 1848 there were few if any female children to be seen.

It affords me heartfelt gratification to be able to give so satisfactory a statement of the suppression of the Meriah sacrifice in Goomsur, Boad, Chinna Kimedy, Jeypore, Calahundi, and Patna, though it would be as injudicious as impolitic to leave them to themselves for some years to come.

These countries are almost blank spaces on the map, which affords as little aid in tracing the course and extent of the operations I have described, as it did in directing my often tedious and toilsome marches.

It is not without pain that I refer, ere I conclude, to the unceasing and bitter oppo-

sition I encountered shortly after my return
from China and my appointment as Agent
to the Governor-General, in supercession
of Captain Macpherson. Not only did the
most violent articles appear almost daily in
the press, frightfully distorting all my acts,
and causing much alarm to the Government—but in the very country which was
the scene of my operations, men were employed to propagate 'and foment all kinds
of false reports, and this, too, in a country
just recovering from the throes of a rebellion. How I was hindered and harassed
by these malignant reports I need not now
relate. Happily I triumphed over these
difficulties, and by the kind permission of
Lord Dalhousie, I published an answer to
a tissue of gross misrepresentations, which
appeared in the " Calcutta Review," and
since then all opposition ceased.

Increasing ill-health warned me that I must seek some relaxation from this wearing climate. I felt that I had accomplished my mission, and that I might now withdraw. I had been cheered in my labours by the unvarying support of the Government I served, and I have recorded in an Appendix some of these marks of approval.

I left the Hill tracts of Orissa with unfeigned sorrow, but I was the more reconciled to this necessity, as my able and zealous Assistant, Captain Macviccar, had rejoined me from England, and was prepared to take my place.

APPENDIX.

APPENDIX.

ONE special object in printing the following orders, letters, &c., is to shew that from the very outset of my connexion with the Khond country, I enjoyed the confidence of superior authority. From the Honourable Mr. Russell, General Taylor, Sir Frederick Adams, Lord Tweedale, Lord Hardinge, Lord Dalhousie, and the late Court of Directors of the East India Company, I received the following expressions of approval.

I have thought it might not be un-
interesting to reprint an article published in
one of the Local journals long after I had
quitted India.

*Extract from Division Orders by General
G. A. Taylor, Commanding Northern
Division, dated Waltair, 10th June, 1834.*

The command of the troops in Kimedy
suddenly devolved upon Captain Campbell,
41st Regiment, at a very critical period,
and when the state of affairs required active
zeal, intrepidity, and judgment. Captain
Campbell on this occasion as on many subsequent ones, when in command of his regiment, has proved he possesses these valuable
qualities in an eminent degree.

———

*Copy of a Letter from General Sir
Frederick Adams, Governor of Madras,
dated 26th June, 1834.*

Dear Sir,
I have had most sincere gratification in
reading the high and well deserved en-

P

comiums passed upon your zeal, energy, and ability by the Commissioner, Mr. Russell, and by Brigader-General Taylor, during the long and arduous service in which you have been engaged in the Circars. Praise from such men is worth ambition, and much do I feel gratified in saying I believe it is entirely merited.

It is a matter of very sincere regret that I have it not in my power at this moment, and under the operation of the existing regulations, to show some more substantial proof of the estimate I have formed of your merits, than can be conveyed by mere words; but be assured that my intention of doing so is most sincere, and I only wait for an opportunity to give adequate proof of my desire to evince it.

Extract from General Orders, Madras Government, 1st July, 1834.

The 41st Regiment deserves particular

notice. This was the only corps employed in Kimedy at the commencement of the insurrection of the Hill Chiefs, and not only afforded effectual protection to the inhabitants, and enabled them to secure their crops from the ravages of the insurgents, but made successful attacks on several of their strong posts before the arrival of any reinforcement. Since the formation of the Brigade, it has constantly been actively employed in co-operation with the other troops. Captain Campbell, who succeeded to the command of the corps on the lamented death of Major Baxter, has greatly distinguished himself by his firm and judicious conduct at that critical period, and by the ability and energy he has evinced on all occasions of active service.

Extract from a Letter addressed by the Honourable G. E. Russell, Esq., Commissioner, to the Chief Secretary to Government, Fort St. George, dated 12th August, 1836.

Meanwhile letters arrived from Captain Campbell, conveying the gratifying assurance that all was well at Oodingherry. On approaching it, a large body of Khonds were observed within a few hundred yards of the camp, who as he advanced came forward with the evident intention of attacking his party. A canister shot from the howitzer failed to do any execution, but Captain Campbell gallantly charging with his little band of six troopers, killed ten men and took one prisoner, which so intimidated them, that they never afterwards ventured to show themselves in any numbers. The men who fell, resisted to the last, and one of the trooper's horses, or rather a horse lent by Captain Campbell, was killed by an arrow.

———

Extract from General Orders by the Government of Madras, dated 4th March, 1837.

The Right Honourable the Governor in Council considers Mr. Stevenson, the Collector and Magistrate of Gangam, and Captain Campbell of the 41st Regiment N.I., at first Secretary to the Commission, and afterwards Assistant to the Collector and Magistrate of Gangam, to be entitled to high commendation for their zealous and efficient co-operations with the Honourable Mr. Russell on all occasions.

———

Extract from a Minute of the Honourable Mr. Russell, dated 19th January, 1838.

Captain Campbell has acquired a know-

ledge of the country and people of the
Hill Tracts in the Gangam District under
circumstances never likely to occur again;
and his local experience and personal influence with the different Hill chieftains give
him an advantage over any other person
who could be appointed to the situation of
Principal Assistant to the Commissioner.
My acquaintance with Captain Campbell
commenced during the military operations
in Kimedy, and all I have seen of him has
been on service. I' will not say that I
have no private feelings towards him, for
no one who knows his value as a public
officer can do otherwise than feel an interest in him; but I can with truth declare
that the opinion I have stated is founded
on public grounds only.

———

*Extract from the Minutes of Consulta-
tion, Madras Government, dated 27th
January, 1838.*

The testimony borne by the Honourable

Mr. Russell to the merits of Captain Camp-bell, and the peculiar qualifications posess-ed by him for the projected office of Principal Assistant to the Commissioner in Goomsur, is as creditable to that officer as it is satisfactory to Government, and the recommendation submitted therein for his appointment to that office will receive favourable consideration.

Extract from the Minutes of Consultation, Madras Government, dated 14th March, 1838.

The Right Honourable the Governor in Council has observed with much satisfac-tion the great success which has attended Captain Campbell's exertions to suppress the practice of Human Sacrifice in the Goomsur Maliahs, which is considered to be very creditable to that officer.

Copy of a Letter from the Agent in Gangam to the Chief Secretary of the Government, of Madras dated 28th October, 1841.

Sir,

I have the honour to request that you will lay before the Right Honourable the Governor in Council the accompying letter dated the 26th inst., addressed to me by Major John Campbell, 41st Regiment, N.I., my Principal Assistant, intimating his wish to join his regiment in the event of its being destined for active service in China.

In submitting this communication, it may be permitted me to express my acknowledgment of the very valuable assistance I have received from Major Campbell during the last four years, and my regret should the exigencies of the public affairs in other quarters cause the temporary withdrawal of his service from this District.

Extract from a Letter from the Honour-able Court of Directors, dated 17th June, 1846.

Consequent upon disturbances in the Golcondah District, and the great want of available troops in the Northern Division, the immediate movement of the 41st Regiment from Palavcram to Vizagapatam by sea was ordered. Notice the alacrity displayed on the occasion, which is considered highly creditable to Lieutenant-Colonel Campbell, and the 41st Regiment, as well as to all the departments concerned.

———

Remarks by the Most Noble the Marquis of Tweedale, Governor and Commander-in-Chief, Madras.

Although all departments concerned

used their utmost to accelerate the embarkation of the corps, to Colonel Campbell, C.B., is due the credit of having the wishes of Government carried into effect so promptly, as he never made a difficulty from first to last.

———

Extract from a Letter from the Secretary to the Government of India, to Lieutenant-Colonel J. Campbell, C.B., Agent in the Hill Tracts of Orissa, dated 12th February, 1849, with reference to the Campaign against Ungool.

I am directed to inform you that the Right Honourable the Governor-General in Council considers that you have conducted the duty with which you were charged in a manner highly satisfactory ; and His Lordship in Council desires me to convey to you the thanks of the Government for the promptitude and decision with which this service has been performed.

———

Extract from a Letter from Secretary to the Government of India, with the Governor-General, dated 28th April, 1849.

In reply, I am directed to observe that the Governor-General considers this Report as a very sensible and most satisfactory one, and to request that you will convey to Lieutenant-Colonel Campbell the Governor-General's approbation of the firmness, skill and judgment which he has displayed in the performance of the arduous duties committed to him, and to assure him of the lively satisfaction which His Lordship has experienced in learning the full and happy results of his exertions.

From F. J. Halliday, Esq., Secretary to the Government of India, to Lieutenant-Colonel J. Campbell, C.B., Agent in the Hill Tracts of Orissa, dated 16th June, 1849.

SIR,

I am directed to acknowledge the receipt of your letter dated the 31st ultimo, with its enclosure, and in reply to assure you of the great regret with which the President in Council has learnt that the state of your health compels you to resign your appointment. During the period you have been at the head of the Agency for the Suppression of the Meriah sacrifice, the Government have had every reason to be satisfied with the progress which has been made towards the extinction of that rite, and equally so with the commencement which you have made in the adoption of measures for the suppression of the crime of female infanticide. Your proceedings have always

appeared to be judicious, and well adapted
for effecting the great end in view, and
from your continuance at the head of the
Agency, the Government had confidently
anticipated the early and complete extirpa-
tion of the Meriah rite within the limits
of the tract of country under your super-
vision.

———

*From George Couper, Esq., Under-Secre-
tary to the Government of India, dated 3rd
March, 1854.*

SIR,

I am directed to acknowledge the receipt
of Colonel Campbell's letter, dated the 9th
ultimo, and in reply to convey the expression of the satisfaction of the Governor-
General in Council, at the results as therein
reported of the operations of the Orissa
Agency during the past season.

From F. F. Courtenay, Esq., Private Secretary to the Most Noble the Governor-General of India, to Major-General Campbell, C.B., dated 11th April, 1855.

Lord Dalhousie desires me to express to you his regret at learning that the state of your health is such as to cause the loss to the Government of India of services which he has frequently had occasion to appreciate so highly, and approve so cordially, as those which you have rendered in the Hill Tracts of Orissa.

———

The following observations are extracted from a despatch from the Honourable the Court of Directors, dated 14th June, 1854, and were forwarded to the Head-Quarters of the Agency, after my departure, by the Secretary to the Government of India, who stated that the Governor-General, Lord Dalhousie, felt assured that the Agency

would receive with satisfaction this appro-
ving testimony emanating from the highest
authority.

" In conducting the operations, and dealing with the rude inhabitants of the country, the officers of the Agency have experienced no ordinary difficulties, and appear
to have shewn a wise discretion and a clear
perception of the best method to secure
success. They have maintained an attitude
of firmness, without unnecessary resort to
forcible measures. They have calmed
angry feelings by conciliation, and have
opposed rational persuasion to popular prejudice and error. They have substituted
confidence by temperate explanation in personal conferences. The means of conciliation have been so well directed in the majority of instances, as not only to overcome
the opposition, but to obtain the co-operation of the leading men.

" Viewing the Meriah operations as a
whole, they have been highly successful,

and are creditable to the officers concerned; nor is it in measures of repression alone that we see cause for present satisfaction and future hope.

" It is obvious that the germs of an ultimate civilization have been planted in the country, and we may entertain a confident hope that the advance of the population towards a higher social condition, will be in an accelerated ratio of progress."

Human Sacrifices in Orissa.

Extracted from " Friend of India," dated September 28th, 1854.

All over India the warfare against the darker crimes is everywhere proceeding, and everywhere successful. Mr. Gubbins at Agra, Mr. Montgomery at the Punjab, and Mr. C. Raikes everywhere, are weaning the people from their habit of infanticide. Though thuggee by poisoning still flourishes, thuggee in its traditional form may be considered almost extinct. Captain Hervey at Bombay pursues the criminal tribes who wander over the Western Presidency. Mr. Jackson in Bengal is enlarging the sphere of his operations against the Dacoits, and his hands will speedily be strengthened. Finally Colonel Campbell reports from Orissa the almost entire suppression of the practice of offering human victims, once as prevalent in Khondistan as in Carthage. In every one of these cases it must be remembered that the crime has been attacked by a special agency, armed with exceptional powers, and backed by laws which recognize the principle, that crime is deserving of punishment and not of impunity.

Hitherto the difficulties in the way of the Government of India have been almost entirely moral. Thuggee as well as infanticide have flourished almost entirely through the deadness of the moral sense, and of the natural affections. They were not regarded

Q

as crimes by those who committed them, and like drunkenness in England, required preventive, even more than retributive legislation. In Bombay, the difficulty with the criminal races is the hereditary character of the tribes, who, like the gipsies in Europe, consider theft and fortune-telling as their natural occupations, the work they were born to do. Even in Bengal, the great cause of dacoity is the cowardice of the people, who are afraid either to cut down the dacoit, or to bear testimony against him. In Orissa, there were, in addition to these moral impediments to improvement, a physical one of no small magnitude. The Khonds are not only dead to all sense of their crime, and confident that it is directly sanctioned by the deity, but they also dwell in fastnesses, which it is scarcely possible to invade. The moral obliquity which protects the White-boy in Ireland, and the physical circumstances which guard the banditti in Calabria, are here united, and in their most impracticable form. Legislation is useless among a people without the pale of law. Threats are absurd where they cannot be enforced even by a campaign. Bribery is powerless when the people believe a crime to be their greatest earthly gain, and moral suasion seems impracticable when applied to races who would consider a Missionary an acceptable offering to the Gods. The British Government, if placed in such circumstances, would probably employ force, as it has done on the coast of Africa, or let crime and people perish together, as in some parts of the continent of Australia. The Indian Government has not adopted either course. It has neither shut its eyes to a fearful crime, or attempted to bring wild tribes back to humanity by wholesale slaughter. A succession of Agents, trained in the school of Indian Politicals, have, for twenty-five years, steadily brought the moral influence derived from irresistible physical strength to bear upon the crime.

We have no intention of passing again over ground already familiar to our readers. Still less are we about to re-open the controversy as to which of three able officers may have obtained the greatest measure of personal success. We confine ourselves strictly to an analysis of the measures adopted for the suppression of the crime, and the degree of success that has been attained. The infected district stretches down the coast from the borders of the Orissa mountains far into Madras, over a territory as large as Wales. The country, itself semi-independent, forms part of two Presidencies, and it was not till 1845 that the Government centralized their operations by the creation of a separate agency.

From that moment the practice of human offerings rapidly declined. Every clan obeys its own chief, and every chief found it advantageous not to be at war with the great Empire beyond his borders. Here was at once a ground of influence. Every chief was informed that his favour from the British Government, depended entirely upon his efforts for the suppression of human offerings. The majority consented, but their promises were broken, and the people, who are convinced their temporal welfare depends upon the practice, were as indignant as Tetzel when his indulgences were denounced. In some districts they became turbulent. Their chiefs were pro· tected from their wrath, their country was opened by rough jungle paths, and they themselves were overawed by bodies of troops traversing their most inaccessible jungles. In other districts, numbers of children purchased for slaughter, are intended to labour as slaves, and the purchasers fancied they would lose money while incurring vengeance from above. Their fears were quieted, and as soon as sound guarantees were obtained for the victims' lives, the boys were left to labour. In some places again, young women were retained by the chiefs as concubines, and afterwards sacrificed to the gods. The chiefs were persuaded to marry them, and thus put an end to all danger of their lives.

All victims preparing for sacrifice were demanded, and usually conceded, and during 1852-53, in only one instance was it necessary to employ the ultima ratio of force. Even in this case Colonel Campbell was attacked before he permitted his men to fire, and this solitary act of severity has produced the best effects. The determination of the Government, maintained for half a generation, the incessant visits to the hills, and the surveillance which amid a passive or discontented population is almost marvellous, have convinced the mountaineers that resistance is impossible. Right or wrong, with their creed or against their creed, the practice must be abandoned. It is abandoned accordingly. In Boad where the slaughter of children was carried to an extent we are almost afraid to record, where bits of flesh cut from the

living man were strewed on the field as a
miraculous manure, where the land, so to
speak, was guanoed with human blood, the
practice has ceased to exist. In the
Chinna Kimedy mountains, it is also
suppressed, and Colonel Campbell thus
records the existing sentiment of the
people:—

" Each chief was invited freely to express
his sentiments on this important subject,
which many did without hesitation, saying,
that when we first came among them they
were like beasts in the jungle, doing as their
fathers had done before them; they now
clearly comprehended that our only object
in coming was to stop human sacrifice; not
a fowl or any thing else was taken, not
even a fence was injured by the people of
the camp, their fields produced crops as
good as formerly, and sickness was not
more prevalent; it was no use resisting
the orders of the Sircar; their Meriahs had
been all removed, moreover they cost much

money, and they were now of one mind
determined never more to have anything
to do with human sacrifice. In two or
three places it was asked, 'what shall we
say to the deity?' they were told to say
whatever they pleased, when the spokes-
man repeated the following formula. 'Do
not be angry with us, O Goddess! for
giving you the blood of beasts instead of
human blood, but vent your wrath upon
that gentleman who is well able to bear it;
we are guiltless.'"

Nor is that all. The very source of the
crime has been attacked. The people have
become convinced that famine does not
follow the abolition of the practice. They
have been relieved of a severe money pres-
sure caused by the purchase of the victims.
They are entering more and more into the
commerce of the plains, and are cultivating
every year a wider breadth of ground.
Finally, we would fain believe that degraded
as these tribes have been, the natural

instinct which forbids the shedding of unnecessary blood, and the natural affection which makes men guard their young, are recovering their force. To sum up, in eighteen years a crime worse than any known in Europe has been eradicated— twelve hundred and sixty human beings have been preserved from a horrible death—an entire people has been induced to forego a crime sanctioned alike by antiquity and by superstition—and a district as large as Wales has been raised a whole grade in the career of civilization. All this has been effected by a Government declared to be oppressive, and by the class whom India honours, and England stigmatizes as Politicals.

We have but one word to add. Colonel Campbell has been concerned in these operations from the first. His firm gentleness has made them successful in the end. He has spent no small portion of a life away from civilization, and in a scene where his efforts have been honoured only by philanthropists. Had he destroyed in battle the number he has saved from immolation, he would have received honours, which should not be denied only because of his modest appreciation of his own success.

THE ,END.

www.ingramcontent.com/pod-product-compliance
Lightning Source LLC
Chambersburg PA
CBHW030818020726
47499CB00006B/1973